EVEN ANIMALS ARE MACHINES / ANDRÉS VACCARI

'I was initially exposed to Andrés Vaccari when I read his innovative collection *Hypercapitalism and Other Tales of Planetary Madness*. The style and force of his writing stuck with me, and in *Even Animals Are Machines*, he further establishes himself as an author who takes concerted risks while remaining in command of his authorship and his ability to tell a good story. Combining flights of theory and *flux schizophréniques* of fantasy, Vaccari has produced what so few writers have done in spite of their best efforts: a work of *genuinely original and literary science fiction*.'

> —D. Harlan Wilson, author of *Dr Identity*, *Outré* and *Nietzsche: The Un-manned Autohagiography*

'Crafted with the same precision and care as the fabulous automaton that is its narrative engine, *Even Animals Are Machines* is a rare novel of philosophical ideas that also tells an engaging story—luminous, melancholy and charged with real soul.'

> —Christopher Brown, Philip K. Dick Award-nominated author of *Tropic of Kansas* and *A Natural History of Empty Lots*

'Vaccari's retelling of the infamous fable about Descartes' mechanical daughter is a marvellous blend of historiography and provocative allegory.'

> —Paul McAuley, author of *Four Hundred Billion Stars*, *Fairyland* and *Beyond the Burn Line*

EVEN ANIMALS ARE MACHINES

Andrés Vaccari

WANTON SUN

Published in 2024 by Wanton Sun

Melbourne, Australia

www.wantonsun.com

ISBN 978-0-6456543-0-1

Design and typesetting by Matthew Revert.

First published in Spanish as *La pasión de Descartes* by Editorial Bärenhaus, 2019. Translated by Andrés Vaccari.

For Xavier and Fabiana

Allow your thoughts to venture for a moment beyond this world and see another, wholly new world in the imaginary spaces of the mind. Suppose that God creates again in this space so much matter that we cannot perceive an empty place in any direction our imagination may extend. Although the sea is not infinite, those who are on a ship in the middle of it seem to be able to extend their gaze to the infinite, and yet there is more water beyond what they can see.

—René Descartes

1

Where Francine Descartes is rescued from the sea by a kind gentleman, architect of the play.

Glimmers from the sailors' eyes leave trails in the grey firmament, like comets of ill omen. Grimaces of fear and fascination detach from their faces, drifting across the surface of the enraged sea. Among the tumult, disfigured by the watery prism, she seeks the sketch of a familiar form.

'Mon père?'

She tries to scream his name and her mouth fills with brackish, icy water. The torrent enters her body and courses through it, filling it completely. The weight drags the girl down.

'Pater, pater. Ut quid dereliquisti me?'

Vortices blur the world into darkness, and the memory of her father's voice reaches her.

It is as though I have fallen into a deep vortex that throws me from side to side without being able to touch the bottom or swim to the surface.

A mute flash of lightning shatters the sky for the last time, and the sea draws her to its bosom of stone, far from the hatred and stupidity of men. Far from her father.

Wrapped up in a peaceful, endless night, she closes her eyes and crosses her hands on her belly, mimicking the dead at rest. She welcomes her fate as papa would have advised, stripping herself of all passion. His voice returns, as though lulling her to sleep.

Someday we will be together again, and nothing more will separate us. Soon there will be a new star in the sky, the star of your soul that will accompany me for the remaining nights of my life.

Judging by the stillness of her eyelids, she has abandoned herself to death—to the idea of death. Things without form lurk in the half-light of her imagination, rough movements, echoes of screams and blows. In her mind, her body sways to the beat of the waves, even though there is no more sea or darkness. The thunder rolls on but no longer provokes fear, having acquired a flat, hollow quality.

The girl opens her eyes. She is lying on a smooth, grey-stone floor in the middle of an infinite platform. With her drenched white nightgown and golden halo of hair, she could be a Medusa dragged from the ocean floor. She props herself up on her elbows, swallowing air, as though she has just learned how to breathe.

She is not alone, wherever she is. Twenty paces away, a tall, broad-shouldered man stands in the gloom. With a circular motion, his forearm drives the crank of a cylindrical machine supported on four wooden feet. A drum rotates on its axis. Inside the drum, rocks and sand produce the sound of thunder and rain.

It is but a glimpse until her sight clouds over. Water flows from her eyes, tracing streams on her cheeks. She appears to be crying, profusely.

The storm ceases with a last creak, and the air carries a whiff of burnt gunpowder. The man takes his walking stick and approaches her, limping slightly. His face is long and narrow, with a prominent nose and deep eyes. His goatee and moustache are as thin as the strokes of a quill. He wears a short-skirted doublet, breeches, flared black-silk trousers, polished riding boots, a sleeveless waistcoat, and a black coat with gold buttons and forked tail down to his knees. His unstarched shirt is bright red with a discreet lace ruff. The attire is completed by a bandolier and a broad-brimmed hat with silk flowers.

The man removes the hat and leans before her, taking her hand. He does not wear a wig and his hair is jet-black, curled in perfect ringlets.

'With your permission, damoiselle.' His resonant voice shakes the girl. Her hand looks pale and small in the embrace of those knotted, dark fingers. 'Welcome back to terra firma, my Empress.'

The girl, about twelve, stands on her feet and expels a stream of water through her mouth. 'Merci monsieur, whoever you are.'

'You do not have to treat me formally, my dear. Your spirits are very agitated on account of what has preceded, and this has affected your ability to remember. I am Señor Vicente de la Vega, at your service.'

He puts on his hat and gestures towards the stage, a hulk about ten metres wide and three metres high. 'That was the conclusion of the play, also its beginning.'

The scenery represents a stormy sea. Parallel rows of wooden waves sway along the stage. A toy ship bops up and down, disappearing to the right. The momentum of the mechanisms is exhausted, and the scene comes to a standstill.

'Who are those men? Why do they want to destroy me?'

'Brutish sailors, damoiselle. You must not worry about them anymore. Right now, our most pressing duty is to attend to your well-being. We must hurry before you catch a fatal cold.'

'Tell me, monsieur, is this Heaven? Do I deserve Heaven? Me, a creature without a soul.'

'I see you are beginning to remember!'

'With all due respect, you do not look like an angel.'

'Don't be afraid of my appearance! For I am your faithful friend and servant. I fear there is no Heaven or Hell for us. Anyway, we do not have time to delve into metaphysical questions. There is a lot of work to do!'

De la Vega walks to the side of the stage, leaning his stick against a hatchway. He pulls a thick rope with both hands and the curtains on the opposing wings begin to unfold. The light fades as the curtains are drawn until all that is left is penumbra, one breath away from complete darkness.

Resting his weight on the cane, de la Vega bows before her. He offers his arm, and the girl accepts. He leads her into the dark, skilfully deploying the cane to conceal his bad leg. With her skirts tucked into her hand, it is an effort to follow him. The Señor's perfume is sweet and sharp, like the aroma of a good cognac.

'Unlike those simple and ignorant people, you are reserved the most important role in the play.'

'All I remember are confusing things. They seem to be the memories of someone else.'

'They are indeed, my princess, but before you worry about them, you must recover, lest the damp spoil those exquisite mechanisms in which so much art has been invested.'

She perceives in the darkness the silhouettes of other stages scattered throughout the immense enclosure. Above their heads—in gaping vaults spaced at regular intervals—a network of ropes, pulleys, beams and counterweights supports angels, crowds, tigers, forests, lightning rays, mountains and gods. Oil lamps hang from long chains, projecting a grid of diffuse, criss-crossing shadows.

They stop in front of another platform, and de la Vega disappears behind the curtains. She hears the sound of pulleys, and the light around her grows in intensity. The curtains open to reveal a rectangular room with low ceilings pierced by thick wooden beams.

The most prominent object on the stage is an iron stove encased on the wall. It is adorned with raised floral patterns and features a ceramic column adjoined to the ceiling. There is a bed, two chairs and a small desk. De la Vega helps her to climb the steps. The stage is narrow, and she realises that its apparent depth is the product of a trompe-l'œil canvas in the background.

The gentleman heads straight to the stove and opens the hatch. With the iron handle, he scrapes the flint and the flame lights on the third attempt. The girl notices the personal objects on the desk and bed: a leather bag, a green hat with an orange feather, a compass, writing implements, a sheathed sword, a bottle of perfume. The objects seem to await the imminent return of their owner.

De la Vega urges her to come closer. She extends her arms in front of the stove, closes her eyes and lets the warm glow filter inside, restoring her body. As he prepares a concoction in a bronze pot, his expression changes. When he looks at her, his eyes fill with sadness and compassion.

A bell peals in the distance, and she counts four strokes. De la Vega has disappeared. The pulleys screech again, and a wooden slat descends, suspended from two ropes, carrying garments and bags.

'I'll draw the curtains and come back in a moment to finish the necessary details.' His voice seems to come from everywhere at once. 'You will have complete privacy. Do not drink from the pot yet. The infusion is very hot.'

She counts the dresses, caressing the fabrics in her fingers: silk, velvet, taffeta, lace. 'Quatorze, quinze…'

Her eyes fill with scarlet and yellow, crimson and vermilion, each material giving rise to a unique shudder.

From the bags, she takes a chemise of thread, a pair of black slippers, white socks and a Chinese fan as long as her forearm. She manages to loosen the bodice, removing the gown and skirts with difficulty. She roughly strips away her stockings and chemise, as if struggling against a drunken suitor.

The girl is not so much naked as uncovered. The surface of her limbs and upper body is a flexible material. Resembling finely carved ivory, it is a perfect mimicry of human skin. The lower torso, stomach and pelvis expose the mechanisms of an automaton. A network of ducts can be seen, some as thick as veins, others as thin as threads. Small elastic receptacles contract and dilate, impelling the movements, sensations and ideas of the machine through the bundles of tubes.

Once the stockings and chemise are in place, the girl becomes a natural creature again. The illusion is masterful, and she is more perfect than reality because she is indifferent to death.

The young woman puts on her clothes and slippers. She has chosen a doublet of crimson taffeta with bluebell flowers and fanciful branches embroidered in silver. The dress has sewn-on valances of scarlet velvet and wide skirts of ochre silk. Only the cords on the back need adjusting.

Once dressed, she returns to the stove. She unfolds the Chinese fan, revealing the figure of a majestic peacock with splayed feathers. A sigh of pleasure and surprise escapes her throat. Her gaze flickers across the stage to the desk, where she discovers a half-finished letter among the writing instruments. With a quick and accurate movement, she takes it between her fingers and reads.

I'll be honest about my project. What I want to produce is not something like the Ars Brevis *of Lull, but a completely new science that will provide the general solution to all possible equations with any kind of quantity.*

The bell interrupts her reading, six chimes this time, followed by the voice of de la Vega rumbling through the air.

'Are you done, damoiselle?'

'You can come in.'

She hears boots treading on the wooden steps. Upon seeing her, de la Vega performs an exaggerated bow, catching his hat before it slides to the ground.

'Oh, my eyes should not deserve to contemplate such beauty. It is as though you cast your own light!'

'You are a shameless sycophant, but continue if you wish. As Cervantes said, there is no woman in the world who does not like to be told that she is beautiful.'

'Ivory from Morocco, crystals from Venice, refined rubber shipped from the Portuguese kingdoms in America—but you, my princess, are so much more than the sum of your parts.'

The girl smiles and perfectly circular blushes form on her cheeks. With a broad gesture, the gentleman points to one of his sleeves, then the other, demonstrating that nothing is hidden there. He shakes his hands theatrically and a heavy hand mirror, forged in silver with ruby inlays, flips from out of nowhere.

Applauding the trick, she accepts the mirror with a bow. She marvels at her image. Her fingertips brush against her lips, forehead, eyelids. The effort of her gaze reveals an idiosyncrasy. She is cross-eyed. When the girl focuses on nearby objects, her left eye leans slightly towards the tip of her nose.

After obtaining her permission, de la Vega adjusts the loose ribbons and cords at the back of her dress, then attends to the brew cooling at the foot of the stove. He pours a quantity into a wooden cup and passes it to her.

De la Vega takes care of her hair. With a comb made of bone, he untangles and smooths it out. The golden threads glimmer.

'These hands may seem coarse, but they confer me a manual skill superior to that of the most talented craftsman.'

Drinking in silence, she observes his work in the mirror. Once her hair has been properly prepared, he separates six handfuls of equal thickness and interlaces them.

'What is my name?' the girl asks.

De la Vega stammers, as though struggling to remember.

'Francine,' he says. 'Your name is Francine Descartes.'

He collects the braids on a bun and fastens it with an ornamental comb.

She savours the sound.

'Francine Descartes.'

He retrieves three necklaces from the porcelain box and shows them to her. Without hesitation, she chooses a choker of tiny pearls that fits around her neck to perfection.

'That is correct. You are Francine Descartes, the main character of our play.'

2

Where the great work is unveiled to the fortunate reader, dealing with the life of a famous philosopher who decided to go in search of the Truth.

They leave the stage without further ceremony. They cross puddles of twilight and negotiate areas of varying darkness from penumbra to the dead of night. The man's gentle limping lends rhythm to their walk. They could be dancing through the extension.

He gestures with his free hand, indicating the devices that lurk around them like crouching beasts. 'Here are the curtains and the frameworks opening to many possible scenarios, an unimaginable variety of scenes and amusements.'

They hear a murmur, the muddy rumour of a crowd rising in distinctness—and music! Interlocked melodies ascend and descend, meeting unexpectedly to form beautiful harmonies. Francine's footsteps falter but de la Vega keeps a steady course.

'I must confess, Francine, that after many years of working here, I often wonder if we ourselves are not the real show. In this darkness, as thick as that which separates the stars in the universe without end, I sometimes think I can distinguish the silhouette of a face or hear the echo of laughter. At other times, the silence itself seems expectant, as though composed by the hum of hundreds of lungs holding their collective breath. Once, in the corner of my eye, I thought I saw a yawn!'

He must raise his voice above the racket, yet the effect seems deliberate.

'What a miserable silence life would be without the play! After all, my admired Francine, what is the world but an entertainment to distract God from the boredom of an empty eternity?'

Ahead of them, there is a shape. It is the back of a false wall supported by a wooden scaffold. The structure extends to the right as far as the eye can see. As soon as they peek beyond, the chatter and music cease. Francine spots a multitude of actors, in various poses and attires, framed against different painted backdrops.

De la Vega guides her through the tableaux vivant. The first shows a pastoral scene: a landscape of soft green hills and fluffy clouds sprinkled on a deep blue sky. A group of seven male actors drink jugs of beer, some standing, others sitting on the artificial grass. All are dressed in black coats and hats, white ruffles and sleeves, and soft boots.

Francine's laughter is a translucent gurgling. She quickly covers her mouth with her hands, ashamed of the sound. The actors share certain qualities: the shape of their noses, the symmetry of their eyes, a hint of haughtiness in their brows.

The chimes are heard again in the distance. Everyone counts, waiting for the progression to end. 'Huit.'

'Crooks!' de la Vega explodes. 'You have no idea how hard it has been to find these shameless swindlers, these drunkards hauled from the streets of Paris, Lyon, Poitiers, Amsterdam. Do you see there? That curvature of the shoulders? And that nose. Perfect, don't you think, Francine? Yes, each of these evildoers has a shred of truth. That one, there, Philippe I believe is his name, he imprecates exactly like your father. Come on, Philippe! Kindly show us, without offending the ears of our damoiselle.'

Philippe lies on the floor, drunk. A companion, also inebriated, helps him up. Philippe clears his throat with a phlegmatic, overblown cough. He raises a hand to the distant vaults and intones.

'Sacre bleu, mon ami! Please do not send me any more mathematical problems from that pretentious fool. We already have enough toilet paper in the house!'

The girl lets out another laugh and tears flash in her eyes. De la Vega hands her a purple handkerchief.

'With your permission, Francine, we must continue.'

She accepts the handkerchief and his arm, and they resume the march. In the next scene, two men stand in a room with high ceilings and stucco reliefs adorned with floral patterns painted in gold. One wears a black cassock with a belt and head-cap. His partner, twenty years younger, is dressed in silk tights, a loose green shirt, tall boots and a red velvet hat with gold buttons. Noticing the arrival of the spectators, the actors straighten up. Making a grandiose gesture with his arms, the young man recites.

'Then, Polyandre, I will reveal before your eyes the labours of men concerning bodily things. After causing you to wonder at the most powerful machines, the most unusual automata, the most impressive illusions and the subtlest tricks that human ingenuity has conceived, I will reveal the secrets behind these, which are so simple and plain that you will no longer have reason to be amazed at any artefact. I will proceed then to the labours of nature, and after showing you the causes of all her changes, the variety of her qualities and how the souls of plants and animals are different from ours, we will proceed to consider all the things that can be perceived by the senses.'

De la Vega claps dryly.

'Better than the last time! Except for one detail: why do you stand like that? Are you a philosopher or a buccaneer?' Without waiting for an answer, he turns to Francine. 'I must apologise. We are still rehearsing these parts. Now, if it's fine with you, we must hurry. Our hour is about to ring.'

She hurries her step, dizzy at the profusion of colours, clothes and faces that look at her with curiosity—sometimes, she senses, with fear. Then she perceives something at the edge of her vision and stops abruptly in front of a tableau. De la Vega almost loses his balance. Francine's hands unwind without thinking, dropping the fan and handkerchief.

The tableau shows a room in the Dutch countryside. The floor is laid with white and black mosaics as on a chess board, and the walls and furniture are rustic. Through the window, a fake sunlight illuminates the scene with a clear and shadowless light.

There is a man seated in a chair, his back to a desk. He wears a white nightgown and nightcap. Francine sees an armillary sphere, a compass, a ruler and a pile of papers. He is a short man, and his pensive features are already familiar. A girl with long golden hair kneels at his feet, her back to the audience. The man beats out a rhythm with the palms of his hands, alternating between applause and soft blows on his knees.

Clap clap tap tap clap clap clap.

The little girl laughs almost imperceptibly. She imitates the rhythm, faintly, then waits for the next pattern.

Clap clap clap tap tap tap tap clap.

Francine staggers, an outpouring of tears occluding her view of the scene. Her knees sag and de la Vega catches her fall. For a moment, the two balance precariously.

'If it's any consolation, we will return to this scene later.'

De la Vega waves a hand in the air and the music starts again, a string quartet weaving a melody of abstract calm. She dabs at her cheeks to stop the tears. De la Vega lends her another handkerchief, yellow this time. Francine takes it and lets herself be carried away from there. The girl and her father, now immobile and silent like statues, recede behind them.

'Are these my memories? Tell me! What are they doing here, outside my head?'

The bell tolls again, and its ringing never seems to end. She counts the knells. 'Douze.'

'You must be strong, Francine. There is no reason for sadness here, where the love between a father and his daughter lives forever. We have arrived, mon Francine!'

They halt in front of a windowless room with dark walls. The man, now familiar in appearance, sits on a chair wearing a white nightgown. His eyes are closed, and an open book sits on his lap. His hands rest upon the book. Many of the actors, transformed into spectators, have left their assigned places to gather around. De la Vega turns on his heels to address the audience. He taps the ground three times with his cane to garner their attention.

'Ladies and gentlemen! I beg for some crumbs of your time, to give you a divertimento that will not disappoint. We know well that Time is not a generous or kind master, but I promise you that the hours you commend to this work will be a wise investment. What a scandalous comedy is the world! What a devilish and presumptuous mess! But, on the stage, due to the demands of beauty and harmony prescribed by the laws of poetry, the world garbs itself in sense, and dreams become an instrument for the edification of the soul. What you will witness in a moment is the story of a man who set out to find the Truth and unveil the secrets of nature, and of all the adventures and obstacles he encountered on the way. I hope that this modest spectacle will delight you and that, above all, it serves as a sobering fable for our troubled times. Let us go ahead, then!'

They hear a rustling of papers to the side of the stage. A shadow dashes by in the gloom and the figure of a second, hidden person can be distinguished—almost a double of the seated actor. A voice sounds out. Due to the acoustics of the place, it is difficult to determine its origin.

'Several years have passed since I discovered for the first time that, in my earliest youth, I had accepted many false opinions as truths, and that consequently the ideas which I had constructed from these falsehoods were dubious as well. From that moment on, I was convinced of the need to root out my most basic beliefs and begin again, building my idea of the world from the foundations in order to establish firm and permanent truths.'

The light in the scene ebbs and the room sinks into dark. Only the seated man remains, under a luminescence of uncertain origin, like the voice.

'I have now rid myself of all worldly concerns and have sought a secluded place, in solitude, to freely devote myself to the systematic destruction of all my opinions. I will then distance myself from all that can be doubted in the slightest, as if it were absolutely false, and I will continue this way until I find something true or at least until I have understood with certainty that there is nothing true in this world.'

The man on the stage wakens. His deep frown and inward gaze denote a state of deep reflection.

The voice continues.

'In the first place, all that I have hitherto admitted as absolutely certain, I have perceived through the senses. I have discovered that they deceive me from time to time; however, there may be things that cannot be doubted. Like, for example, that I am sitting here by the fire, that I am dressed in a winter gown, that I have this paper in my hands. Can I deny that these hands and this body are mine?'

The thinker raises his right hand and looks at it in surprise.

'Well, I might be dreaming. In examining this possibility, I do not see a sure sign that I can know with certainty whether I am awake or not. However, the things that are represented in dreams are like paintings, made in the likeness of something real and true. Painters, representing mermaids and satyrs, cannot attribute to them completely new forms. They simply mix the limbs of various existing animals. Even if a painter with an extravagant imagination invented something new, such that we would never have seen anything like it, that painter would have to use colours that already exist. In this way, there are simple and universal things that are true and existent, from whose combination are formed all the images of things that reside in our thought, be them true and real or feigned and fantastic.'

The hands of the seated man are uprooted from the body. They rise in the air and float until they disappear in the heights.

Looking around, Francine notices that the whole theatre has been plunged into the deepest darkness. She can hardly see the faces of the spectators. She perceives only the stage, the narrator's voice, the touch of de la Vega's arm, and the uncertain light that illuminates the puppet on the stage that, until a moment ago, had seemed to be a flesh-and-blood actor.

One by one, its quartered body parts rise and twirl through the air until they vanish into the deep space hanging above them. Only the bodiless head is left, suspended in a pool of light.

'I will suppose, then, that some evil genius of extreme power and intelligence has put all his efforts into deceiving me. I will believe that the sky, the air, the earth, the colours, the figures, the sounds and everything external are nothing more than a deception. I will consider that I have neither hands nor eyes nor flesh nor blood, but that I owe everything to a false opinion of mine. What, then, can be regarded as *true?* I, at least—am I not something? But I have denied that I have any senses or a body.'

The head of the meditator begins to gyrate in its place like a spinning top. Francine notices the eyes of the dead puppet. They are wide open and seem to stare at her—and her alone.

'However, there is no doubt that I exist, even if the genium malignum deceives me. It is true that the genium can create illusory worlds as real as our own, but is it not also true that every dream requires a dreamer, and every perception, no matter how false, requires someone to perceive it? So, let the false deity deceive me as much as he wants—he could never make me into *nothing* so long as I thought I was *something*. We must finally conclude that the proposition *I am, I exist* is necessarily true every time I pronounce it or conceive it in my mind.'

The head rises slowly, spinning in space until it disappears.

'Now, I am a true and existing thing. What, then, is what I am? I have already said: a thing that thinks. And what is a thing that thinks? It is a thing that doubts, conceives, affirms, denies, wants, does not want. A thing that imagines and remembers too. And that feels...'

A luminous point appears from where the head had been, expanding into a cloud of soft, enveloping light.

'Are you ready, Francine?' whispers de la Vega. 'Let yourself go. Words and gestures will come naturally.'

Francine can't see the Señor. For her, there is only the light. She glimpses forms and shadows. A little boy running on a prairie. Further away, a rainbow.

The arm of the malign deceiver gently leads her toward the stage, towards the light.

3

Which deals with the tender and terrifying childhood of the wise philosopher René Descartes, and his first reflections on the soul, the body, being and becoming.

And surely, my Lord, before whose eyes the abyss of human conscience is always naked, what could I have concealed in me that I did not want to confess to you? What I would be doing is hiding you from me, not me from you.

—Saint Augustin

The Earth stands motionless in the centre of Creation, and everything revolves around it: the moon and planets, the sun and stars in their crystalline spheres. Down below, the world is a sombre, defective eternity in which nothing returns in the same manner. Earthly bodies draw wandering parabolas and often things go away never to return, like the souls of those who leave the world. Grandmother Brochard says that those souls look from above and that maman is among them.

'She will always be with us, watching us from up there—especially you. One day, we will reunite in Heaven, the abode of God, and you will see her face again.'

At night, the child René looks up at the lights in the sky in search of maman, not knowing which one is her. Some things go away, yes, although they do not vanish completely but subsist mysteriously in new forms. The moon grows night after night until it shines like a sun, then the darkness eats away at it little by little, casting the last sliver of light on the drapery of the sky. Milk becomes cream and butter. The grapes, wine. Wheat, bread. Thrushes appear in the first heat of spring and settle on the trees of the countryside. Their shifting silhouettes resemble living fruits. If you move carefully, you can approach without disturbing them.

When little René looks an animal in the eye, he searches for some glint under the surface of those polished mirrors, something like the thoughts and passions that throb within him.

> 'You see, Francine, that by its own will, the soul can't direct the spirits to those places of the body where the passions are born. It's necessary, then, to think of something else, something that causes the desired passion. Your father often finds comfort in the idea of an eternal and immaterial place where all the people he has loved and lost are waiting for him.'

Jeanne, Yvette, Alphonse, Huguette, Pierre, Claudine.

The names are distant murmurs in the folds of his memory, and the faces slip through the fingers of his imagination to merge into a single face. In the grottoes of memory, Grandma Brochard is the only one who remains motionless like the earth, in that house where he has spent his earliest childhood. What he remembers most clearly are not the names, nor the faces, but the repetitions around which the world finds order: the uncertain patterns, the changing proportions of the worldly.

Just as the actors, when they are called to the stage, put on a mask so that we can't see their faces, I—who am about to climb onto the stage of the world where I have been, until now, a spectator—advance masked.

Every Friday, the enemas are administered and every winter the fevers come. Each morning, little René rises with the same heaviness in his belly, running to the latrine to purge the filthy mud that his body has kneaded in the night of his entrails.

'It's the food that rots, child,' says Huguette, the milkmaid who works at the house. 'It rots inside you. See in that bucket?

See the remains of fish and pumpkin shells? They have been there for days and have become sickening, like everything that dies.'

Then, each year, the green of the leaves returns and the crops reappear. The children rip off their clothes and jump into tubs full of grapes. Covered with dark, sticky juice, they laugh loudly, running to the river to wash before jumping back into the tubs.

The summers return, and on weekends the servants and their families take the tables outside. René, his sister Jeanne—sometimes his brother Pierre—and their cousins sit down for lunch. The light lends solidity, infusing objects with a reality that is clear and cannot be doubted.

When Pierre and father are absent, René deliberately neglects his table manners. Leaning against the back of the chair, he bites the hare's paw noisily and throws the remains to the dogs. Jeanne always behaves correctly. She sits as straight as a column and uses the cutlery to scrape the last shred of meat.

In other ways, they are all too similar. They share the same lost, dreamy look, the same protruding nose as papa, and they walk in the same unhurried, aimless way.

The eternal child runs through the undulating skirts of the meadows and into the woods, searching for the source of the rainbow. His father holds an important job in a distant place where he lives half the year. Whenever he returns, little René does not recognise him.

'This gentleman is our father,' Jeanne must explain. She moves her lips hyperbolically. 'Pa... pa. PA-*PA*.'

Men follow the mandates of the seasons, the same that govern the birds and grapes and all semblances of the eternal. They go, stiff and unfathomable, in their capes and black hats, and when they have become no more than a diffuse memory, they turn up worried and frowning, their clothes loaded with pungent smells. Men spin like the planets and stars, and the routines and activities of the house are ordered around them and their absences. Little

René never wants to know that place from which they return, the world that extends beyond dirt streets, fields, rivers and horizons. When the cold months arrive, it is time to run the pigs. The children surround the animal, and two cousins sit on the creature's back, holding it in place. Alphonse, the oldest servant, speaks sweetly to the animal, caressing its head before plunging the knife into its throat. The animal writhes and emits a deafening screech. Its body gushes dark blood. Each spasm becomes weaker as the heart grows silent until the precise moment when the light in its eyes is extinguished. Of life, only a grimace remains. The creature is only matter now, a *thing* like a rock or piece of wood.

Alphonse makes a longitudinal cut along the belly, and while the children inflate the pig's bladder and kick it into the air, René watches the blood swirling in the bucket. The creature's soul now resides in that bucket, but he knows that it will not become a star because animals do not go to Heaven.

They also bleed little René like a pig. When the fevers and purges return, he fears his life will escape in an effluvium of matter.

'Why,' he asks Doctor Maurait, 'has God created me like this, so weak and imperfect?'

'You are a typical case of melancholy personality. You see, it's the excess of black bile which produces fevers and weakness. God has done nothing wrong. Purges are for your good because sometimes nature needs to be corrected. It needs to be guided by human labour and ingenuity. For that, God created us free, in His image and likeness.'

Much later in life, the memory of Doctor Maurait will continue to jolt him with an involuntary shudder: the black silk cloak, the scrawny fingernails, the crooked beard growing to one side.

René's mother died of tristesse, and he inherited that same tendency, her pale complexion and weak nature. He does not consciously remember her death, but he treasures its impression in an intimate place in his soul.

With the fevers and bleedings come the dreams. He dreams awake and with eyes wide open. Upon awakening, the tide of unconsciousness dumps him on the shores of an intolerable clarity. Pure consciousness, empty of all ideas, can be incomparably more torturous than any nightmare of the body.

The house is cast in a silence of stone, and the child knows that sleep will not come until morning. He draws the lamp close and stirs the flame. His hands intertwine, casting shadows on the wall. He tries to not look at his hands, a trick that forces the illusion to take on a life of its own. Huguette tells him that his pale hands remind her of new-born birds. Small and useless.

'Anyway, you'll never have to use them to work, will you?'

Down here, he reasons, the world is movement, a restlessness of liquids and spirits. Perhaps the only eternal thing is this movement itself.

He invents prayers.

'Dear God, I humbly ask that my poor, ignorant soul be eternal, even if it is a tenuous reflection of Your Eternity.'

He speaks to maman inside his mind.

Where does my soul go when I sleep, maman? Would it be the same place where things go when they hide from the light? There must be another place, a world as real as this one, a reality of no-light. There the thrushes fly when the days become cold, and there goes the green of the leaves in autumn. There life goes when the blood stops stirring. There go the cold baths and Pierre's beatings. There goes the tincture of rose water and vinegar for fevers, chicory root and honey for stomach cramps.

Perhaps things take on other appearances there yet remain the same. Otherwise God would have to create things constantly out of nothing, and every event would be unique and unrepeatable. The morning thrush would not be the same thrush at sunset, and it would never be the same person who sees the sun rise and set, who opens and closes his eyes.

At dusk, during a precious moment of solitude before the servants turn off the lamps, the child looks in the mirror and searches his face for signs of change. He digs into his gaze for that light.

Are you there, dear soul of mine? Are you the same, still with me, or am I someone else today?

4

Which is about the first love of the hero of our adventure, and about death, and God, and other things.

He is a man now, a man who feels old, who maintains the habit of studying himself in the mirror each night after the curtains fall on the world. The darkness completes his solitude, consummating and redeeming it. He prays to God with all his will.

'Our Father who dwells in the Heavens, I beg you to continue upholding the order of the world. You who are everywhere and who are the Good, I beg You and all the Saints that you never let things cease to exist. You are a kind and unalterable God, and my soul is a tiny and sick thing that could never conceive of Your infinite Goodness and Perfection. My body is earth and ash. Do what you want with me, my God. I am Your servant, an imperfect shadow of Your Idea. Receive this soul in your lap when You so dispose. Amen.'

He remembers his father's voice.

All that we have lived is preserved in the soul, and God sees everything because He can read man's soul as if it were a book.

When the dead wake and gather to sit at the right of Christ, René will ask God to allow him to see that book. He wants to see them all once more—his father, wet nurse, uncle, grandmothers, sister—without the aberrations of memory. He wants to see maman and Francine with the transparent eyes of the soul.

He wants to see Claudine.

Shortly after his fifth birthday, they send him to Grandmother Brochard's second house in La Haye. The girl Claudine lives across the street, and her family is very close to the Brochard and Des Cartes families.

Sometimes, when they play, she takes his hand or rests on his shoulder. In her room, as she looks at the marbles and dolls on the floor, the girl's left eye slightly deflects to one side so that each eye seems to look at something different. To René, this imperfection only makes her more beautiful and perfect. He shows her his secret collection of things: rocks, pieces of pottery and glass, lost buttons, dead insects, parts of dolls. Her gaze branches sweetly as she struggles to focus on them.

During the second summer in La Haye, René and Claudine escape together, hiding from the adults and other children. They take advantage of precise gaps in the routines of the house. They discover hiding places, the weeds of the garden, the hollow behind an open door, the space under the stairs, places secluded from the adult gaze.

They stay wherever they are without moving or talking, huddled very close, their heartbeats following restless and uneven rhythms, the world filling with invisible tremors. Next to Claudine, he finds that terror and delight are impossible to pry apart. When she contemplates him, her eyes know that there are two Renés. They understand that we are all something else, uncertain, below the surface.

One day, Pierre appears unexpectedly at grandmother's house and becomes angry with them because they have muddy shoes. He enters, whip in hand. He wears riding boots. He throws off his cloak and a servant takes care of it and the saddle.

René and Claudine have just returned from a morning on the riverbanks. Along the way, they checked the traps René had placed in the forest the previous afternoon. They found a hare, still alive, and Claudine carried it in her arms, cuddling it against her chest, feeling the tingle of its fear. Upon arriving at the river, she released the hare. Claudine always lets the animals go free and René never says anything.

The boy had collected some pebbles. Under the water of the river, the colours appeared bright and alive, but when he removed them from the water they lost their hue, and this disappointed him. The secret is to keep them in a tub of water, but then it would be necessary to hide them lest the servants empty the tub into the garden.

At the house, Pierre asks if they have found any hares and René says 'no'.

'Liar,' Pierre retorts, raising his hand. Claudine starts to cry and soon René tastes his own tears, as though the sadness in their two bodies is one. Pierre forbids René to leave the house.

'After all,' he says, 'I have two sisters!' And he laughs, throwing his head back.

He has been entrusted with the task of making René a gentleman. At meals he studies the manners of his younger brother and corrects him. René must carry his brother's belongings and take them to his room. He must polish Pierre's sword, buttons and boots.

'Papa,' Pierre accuses, 'René plays with the servants' children. It is not appropriate. What manners will he learn? Playing in dirt and mud, running around the farm like an animal, a beast without culture.'

Life improves considerably when Pierre goes to the Collège, visiting them only for Easter and other religious holidays.

After the boy's father and stepmother settle in Rennes, Uncle Ferrand takes care of René's education. Uncle's house in Châtellerault is huge. There are rooms he never enters and stairs he will never climb. Here René feels less free, and the servants walk quietly as though in fear.

Away from Claudine, in his uncle's house, her absence settles into his body. It is an imprecise and constant pain, a shadow that follows him, which his gaze can never catch.

In the mornings and afternoons, René takes reading, writing and diction classes in French and Latin. Uncle Ferrand is absent for long periods. During the holidays, he teaches his nephew fencing and riding. Once the child can ride alone, his uncle leads him to hunt hares and deer in the woods outside the village. René does not want to remember the names of the numerous cousins who visit almost every day.

Jeanne visits on weekends and goes to Mass with them at the local church. The hours stretch sweetly in her company and the world fills with light. The siblings play hide-and-seek and card games. They invent theatre plays, imitating the spectacles they watch in the markets of the main square.

Sometimes they go to their uncle's library, a narrow, windowless room with shelves that take up all the walls. Jeanne is responsible for lowering the books and arranging them on the carpet. There are books on law, anatomy, medicine, optics, astronomy. There are commentaries on the Bible and Aristotle. Many are quickly put back, since they contain no illustrations and are difficult to decipher.

René reads to Jeanne falteringly, translating into French and filling in the words he can't understand with concepts of his own invention. The anatomy books give her nightmares, but these are precisely the ones that interest her brother the most.

There is a particular book that the boy finds fascinating. It is entitled *De humani corporis fabrica*, and its pages exhibit the bodies of dead men sliced open like cattle. The fine craftsmanship of the engravings illuminates the interior of the bodies with pristine light, like that which falls through church windows. The child imagines this light entering his body, that strange and cryptic husk, his most intimate possession and yet a dreadful thing that he wishes, somehow, to cast from himself. The light clears away some of the horror and sadness inside him.

In his memory, an ant crawls across his uncle's palm.

See, René? This ant is wise because it knows its place in the world and carries out God's work without question or understanding. We, on the other hand, are more ignorant than the beasts because, in our arrogance, we believe that we can understand the Lord's designs. The only thing we can know with certainty is that there is a God and that in Him we place our trust, our life and our faith.

His father, grandmothers and uncle teach him that he should pray regularly in the morning, before meals and before going to sleep. René prays much more than he should. He prays after instructions, talking to God secretly and alone. He has developed an active imagination and the habit of dialoguing with himself.

When they go to mass, the child looks for God in the corners of the church, in the images of saints, in the crosses and in the shadows of the stone arches. If God is everywhere, why do they come looking for Him here on holy days?

Uncle Ferrand warns him, in harsh terms, that you must be careful what you say. There are many different ideas about God, and people are willing to kill and die to defend them. René keeps his questions to himself because there is something that he does not understand, something that wants to be a question, maybe many questions, but that cannot be articulated as a definite thought or feeling.

Later, the Jesuits will teach young Renatus the word that classifies what had previously been only a cloudy sensation, an equivocal but nagging presentiment.

Machina.

Scaffolding, support, machine, structure, fabric.

Machina.

Trick, plot, stratagem, scenery.

Machina.

The world is a machine designed by an inconceivable craftsman.

Will God have a face in the darkness that one day will become light?

When René closes his eyes and seeks God in the darkness of his soul, Yvette, his wet nurse, appears to him with her fleshy pale face, her clear and generous eyes. Pierre would beat him up if he discovered that he imagines God with Yvette's face, but one is free there, in the room of the mind where the world is born and made anew according to designs of the will.

It is a freedom as intoxicating as it is terrifying. One can remake all things from scratch, but the soul can also become a prisoner of its own projections. It is like when the wind blows a candle flame and the shadows on the wall stretch out, forming frightening figures.

The servants are more excited than usual, and the dogs have taken to hiding among the weeds in the garden. An important celebration is about to take place. They have set the table in the main room and have brought chairs and chandeliers from other places in the house.

For two weeks, Uncle Ferrand has spent his mornings in the kitchen, inspecting cutlery and dishes, supervising the servants and scolding them terribly when they put things in the wrong place.

Now the day has arrived, and the streets fill with a constant procession of carriages and horse riders wearing black cloaks with wide hats that hide their faces in shadow. Hundreds of Protestants are meeting in Châtellerault with the King's representatives. The thunderous carriages bring from that horizon more and more men in black wearing huge hats.

Esther, the servant, takes the children inside and tells them that they must stay in their rooms. She says that they will not be able to play in the yard nor on the riverbanks nor run on the promenade.

That night, the house on rue Carrou-Bernard is filled with deep and strange voices. The little boy hears fragments of raucous pronouncements coming from downstairs. He walks very lightly through the hallways and tries to capture what the adults are saying. They speak of idolaters and golden statues, of freedoms and claims to the King, of persecution. Above all, they talk of God.

God has no face.

Death likes the warm months. Death likes flowers and invigorated rivers. And there the grandmothers go, and Uncle Ferrand, to the abode of no-light where the flesh transubstantiates into motion.

There goes Claudine, holding the sickly grey hand of the plague. René has never felt so alone and helpless. Before going to Heaven, people spend time in bed, preparing to leave, and the doctor and pastor come to visit them every day. Their bodies turn pale, appear to shrink, and begin to emanate a heavy odour that permeates the air. At night, the rooms where the dead wait are filled with long, yellow shadows.

When his time comes, Uncle Ferrand does not want people to pray for him.

'And don't even think about ringing the church bells!' he yells. 'I'll return from Hell to give everyone a good lunge.'

René knows that his uncle does not believe in Hell, nor Heaven nor Purgatory, because he once told him that. It is one of the many things that he can't tell anyone.

Carefully, René removes his wig, apprehensive of what he might find beneath. With time, his hair has turned silver and the skin around his eyes has withered and wrinkled. This body knows itself tired and nowadays he avoids seeing himself naked. He has learned that there are very few certainties that the mind cannot doubt. However, the world remains the same mystery as always, a deeper mystery than anything that distant child ever suspected. Sometimes the light of Truth only makes us realise the real magnitude of the darkness extending all around.

5

In which the wise philosopher has second thoughts about his joint creation.

> We would be ascribing to the created creature the perfection of the creator if the creature could continue its existence independently of anything else.

—René Descartes

It is time to unveil his creation. Inside the stove's dark interior, it stares into a corner. In the three weeks since Rêver's departure, the machine has been motionless, although he believes he heard it breathing a couple of times. He opens the door and lights its face with the lamp. The girl's features move and change expression in the flickering light, but nothing seems to animate it inside. He presses his ear against its flat, hard chest. He maintains this posture for a few minutes without perceiving sound or movement.

The hostility that he initially felt towards the automaton has dissipated. He'd considered giving it back to Rêver, but his curiosity grew more powerful than his vanity. Perhaps his discomfort arises from the fact that the mechanic ignored many of his specifications. He suspects that Rêver sees the machine as a kind of mockery or defiance. He told the mechanic that technique must be guided by reason and based on the foundations of a true knowledge of the subject, otherwise ars is blind empiria, a mere grope in the dark.

'Descartes,' Rêver replied, 'with all due respect, our purpose is to imitate the actions of the living, not to duplicate its mechanisms as found in nature. God has His mechanics, and we have ours. You said it yourself: the goal of natural philosophy is utility. Therefore, the representations of science must conform to the principles of reason and help us to intervene in nature, without presuming a divine knowledge of it. Our material ideas, the instruments of science, are hypothetical, artificial—just like our daughter! And, as Aristotle taught us well, representation should not be a simple copy of reality but the recreation of life.'

There it is: perhaps the reason is deeper, something close to fear. There are moments when the mind takes some time to correct the erroneous judgment of the senses, when the soul is seduced by the mirages of the body.

In the absence of reason, it is easy to believe that the automaton is she herself, back from Hades.

He, like Orpheus, must avoid looking at her.

They took precautions. Since the beginning of the investigation, the servants have stayed in the house at the back, with the excuse that Descartes and Rêver need space to carry out their experiences. The main house is small and humble, far from the comfort and luxury of Endegeest Castle, where he resided for two years after Francine's departure. This place is more in line with his current needs. Here he feels safe, hidden. His enemies cannot find him. More importantly, neither can his friends. Except for Rêver, of course. He will never be able to hide from Rêver.

He sleeps in his nightgown so as not to appear naked in front of the automaton. It is uncomfortable for him to sleep like that, but once sleep comes it does not matter anymore.

He continues with his experiences and dissections. Progress is painful and there seems to be nothing more to discover. Recently, he invented a way to weigh the air and a method to determine the ratio between the weights of air and water. His servant, Ludolf, brings him hearts, eyes and brains from the butcher. His aide-de-chambre, Pietr, takes care of the chickens and marks the eggs, one stroke for every six hours of incubation.

Descartes removes the eggs in successive stages of formation and takes them to the main room. Observations should be made under direct natural light, and in spring the angle of the ecliptic is optimal.

The effort of looking through the lens causes frequent and intense migraines. Meanwhile, under the eye of the instrument, the tiny automata of nature multiply and retreat from sight. Stripping life from its disguise only reveals more surfaces, an infinite regression of appearances.

God is the vanishing point of the world.

6

Where our beloved masters of ceremonies roam the infinite theatre of the world and witness unfinished fragments of the great play.

'Après tois, Francine. Be careful with the steps. You have been splendid as always.'

Resuming their march, she clings to the arm of the Señor, still disoriented after her interpretation of Claudine and the sudden changes of time and scenery. He sets the pace with his cane. Francine unfolds the fan and, after admiring the blue bird for a moment, waves it vigorously.

As they step into the gloom, the murmur of another crowd reaches their ears. Words flutter in the dark air and pounce on one another, piling up to the point of unintelligibility. Words in various languages express the full range of human passions. The words of lovers, whispered. The imprecations of arguers, spit out in anger. The cries of those who suffer and the laments of those who die. On their approach, the murmurs turn to screams.

They have arrived in a clearing, a pool of intense light, and find themselves immersed in the din of the crowd. The actors wander seemingly at random across the lit surface, practicing their lines. Francine and de la Vega make their way almost without seeing them, although she feels their wary looks on her skin.

De la Vega leads her to the centre of the scene, where they stop in front of an empty area around a large campfire. It is a fake fire that does not emit heat, ingeniously produced with shreds of transparent, shiny paper, stirred by the wind from a hidden machine.

Following an invisible signal, the crowd begins to pack around the fire. A large man stops a few steps from her, his face like clay kneaded by a constant bad humour. He has a pale complexion, and his hair is white and sparse.

'You know that you are a thinking thing, but you don't know what this thinking thing is. How can you prove that a body cannot think, that its bodily movements cannot produce thought?'

The crowd falls silent.

'That's Thomas Hobbes,' the Señor whispers. 'Old blasphemous curmudgeon! He curses like a sailor.'

Francine notices that the object of the grievance is a wrought iron cage suspended from the ceiling by long chains. The paper bonfire licks the bottom of the cage. She skirts the area to get a better view. Inside the narrow cage, seated at a desk, her father writes by lamplight. She must resist the urge to run to him. It would be impossible to reach him up there, and she must remember, too, that he is not really her father.

The actor seems to have noticed Francine's presence. Their glances meet fleetingly, and he promptly diverts his attention back to his papers. On the other side of the circle, a young man, covered with a purple cloak and wearing a red velvet hat, raises his arms towards the cage.

'Renatus Des Cartes is the Archimedes of the century, the Atlas of the universe, a mighty Hercules, the most ingenious Daedalus! His most sagacious mind has cast a mighty light on the designs of Creation, thus undermining the darkness of the centuries. Geometer, physicist, doctor, anatomist, engineer, musician—there is no science that he has not illuminated. He has unravelled the hidden recesses of nature in order to expose them to the light and clarity of reason!'

Next, an exquisitely dressed woman in ample silk skirts and a gold embroidered blouse approaches. The men bow and let her pass. The woman is so beautiful that Francine cannot tear her eyes away from her.

'Mademoiselle,' de la Vega whispers, 'we shouldn't linger. We can't keep our audience waiting. They are getting bored.'

'She must be a princess or a queen.'

'Indeed, she is Princess Elizabeth of Bohemia, for whom your father had a lot of affection and with whom he kept a long and revealing correspondence. A limpid and insightful mind!'

The lady's voice is firm and clear.

'Since the human soul is only a thinking substance, how can it affect the spirits of the body in order to carry out voluntary actions? I can't conceive of the immaterial except as the negation of the material, that is, as that which can never enter a causal relationship with matter. And yet the soul, supposedly rational and purely thinking, can also be affected by the vapours of the body.'

The man in the cage writes furiously. The criticisms no longer seem to hurt him nor the flattery to lift his spirits. He sometimes looks up, catching some fragment of vituperation or praise, and his exhausted gaze returns to the desk. The written pages fly in the air and hover over the crowd. People try to catch them, struggling silently with each other. Some try to preserve the pages, others to destroy them.

A voice rises from the crowd.

'I can't forgive you! In your philosophy, you have done everything possible to be without God. However, you could not help but ask God to set the world in motion with a snap of his stately fingers. After that, you had no more use for Him!'

De la Vega leads Francine away from the fire. An old man rushes to the edge of the circle, pushing those in his way. He wears a long black coat, a tight black cap and a wide, starched collar.

'You are an idol with feet of clay! Descartes, the revered founder of a new sect, famous disciple of the Jesuits, whom many revere as a God fallen from Heaven. Your insidious hoaxes lead to atheism and Hell! Human reason is surrounded by error and sin. Perfect, true and undoubtable knowledge is impossible for men.'

The old man rushes toward the cage. Two other men take him by the arms, holding him back. The man falls to his knees and lets out a wrenching cry of rage. De la Vega and Francine retreat towards the outer edge.

The actors argue among themselves and cast glances in their direction. Halfway through, they run into a group of very striking, odd-looking people, and Francine pulls on de la Vega's arm with both hands, pressing the fan against him. The men are very tall and thin, with pale faces, short hair and geometric beards that she finds very comical. They wear tight suits made of a material that looks like finely spun, unnaturally shiny wool. Some of them carry curious gadgets over their noses—they appear to be wearable lenses placed near the eyes. There are women dressed in loose chemises, very daring, as though they have rushed out from their homes in their underwear. There are even two women wearing pants!

Francine is unsure whether to laugh or run. She does not even understand the language they speak. From time to time, when exchanging observations among themselves, one points to the hanging cage and everyone looks in that direction, nodding in thoughtful agreement.

'Don't worry about them, Francine. We should have taken the longer route!'

'What are they saying?'

'Oh, don't pay attention to them.'

'Come on, I want to know. Do you understand what they are saying?'

'Ah, nothing very interesting. Let me see. They are now saying that, thanks to our dear philosopher, "the subject has become a solitary consciousness without flesh or body, a geometric point that can only access the external world, from which it has been ontologically split, through misleading representations that have no necessary or true relationship with nature". We have discarded these failed scenes from the play. If we wanted to represent reality truthfully and in all its multiplicity, the play would encompass the extension of the world itself—or even exceed it!'

As they leave, a nervous, hunched-over young man with intense eyes approaches them. He wears a strangely cut shirt with no ruffles or sleeves and wrinkled black pants. He wears those strange optical gadgets on his nose and his hair is very short. He looks like a monk or someone sick.

De la Vega raises his cane in warning, but the young man launches into a speech.

'According to Descartes, universals are modes of thought, objective beings that can appear as aspects of individual material substances. However, the terms "quality" and "mode", qua synonyms of "attribute", have a special meaning in article 56 of *The Principles of Philosophy*, where they are applied to variable attributes. And it's not clear whether we should accept an Aristotelian interpretation of species or genera.'

De la Vega pushes the young man with his stick. 'Stand aside. You've bored us enough!'

As they leave, a last audible exclamation reaches them.

'Theologians are like pigs. You pull one of their tails and they all start screaming.'

The silence and mellow light are comforting after so much spectacle. Francine sighs and fans herself again.

'I must beg your apologies for this mess,' de la Vega says. 'Perhaps in the next function we will be able to include some of these acts that we are working on here.'

'Have I really been part of this play?'

'Countless times! And your performance has been commendable. The other actors have a deep respect for you.'

'I haven't noticed. People seem afraid of me, and I can't remember anything, as though I am seeing all this for the first time.'

'Forgetfulness is the most merciful of our defects, the remedy for all resentment and past grief. Imagine if we could clearly remember every moment of our lives! We would certainly go crazy. Well, we have arrived. Are you ready, Francine?'

'I think so.'

7

Where the young philosopher receives an education.

I take for granted that there are three types of thoughts in me: that is, one of mine that springs from my simple freedom and will, and two others that come from outside: one from the good spirit, and the other from the bad.

—Saint Ignatius of Loyola

He thinks, he remembers, memory being a mode of thought. But is he the one who thinks? Are these memories truly his? Or is it the self that invents itself in the act of remembering?

The journey takes place in an eternal twilight. They leave with the first dawn on the Monday after Easter Sunday. Aside from René and Pierre, the party includes two boys returning to the Collège after their holidays, a Jesuit Father and a servant. They are spread over three horses. René has already forgotten their names.

Winter retreats to its den of no-light, and the trees crouch, longing for the arrival of the warm months. They should have left a few weeks ago, but the cold has been fierce. René has been very ill and still feels weak. He hides, as always, the best he can, telling himself that he must be strong, but he's afraid. He doesn't want to go to an unknown place to find himself surrounded by strangers. Pierre tells him that education and discipline will be for his own good, but it seems to René that his suffering only delights his brother.

I must be strong. I must control myself.

He travels behind Pierre in the same saddle. His brother tells him that the road is full of dangers, but they only come across wagons rushing the opposite way and handfuls of travellers on foot or horseback going in both directions. Sometimes, the adults stop briefly to chat with the walkers, then continue north. René can no longer feel his body, not even the pain. He could be an angel, floating. When they speak to him, he barely moves his head. He nods to everything they say.

They stop in Tours to eat, but he is not hungry. By mid-afternoon, he is so weak that they must lay him crossways on the horse. When he wakes, he finds himself in the bowl of a wide valley, surrounded by fields divided into rhomboid patches. Some of the lots are ready for spring planting and others are set for the arrival of grapes, turnips and radishes.

They stop to rest under the shade from a row of dry, flowerless fruit trees. In the distance they see a river and, beyond, the town: a cluster of low buildings from which the church tower sticks out. Pierre gives him a piece of bread and he swallows it quickly, his body grateful this time. The damp, sweet air clears his head and an unexpected peace floods him. The fire of wakefulness blazes brighter until it conquers the darkness and cold.

They resume the march on foot, and soon after they reach a stretch by the river's edge where stones of unusual shapes accumulate. Inspecting them, René discovers that they are petrified fruits, and a sigh of joy escapes him. He has read about this in the books of wonders. He recognises a peach and walks in a crouch, lifting the stones one by one. There are plums, figs and pears.

He has fallen behind without realising it and Pierre comes to retrieve him, giving him a light kick in the butt.

'Stones?' he says. 'We have enough mortuus pondus with you already.'

Pierre now insists on speaking to him only in Latin. René does not think he will ever grow used to it.

Pierre found him a bed in the boarding house where he stays. René will share his room with four older Collège students. When they arrive, a cow and a goat tied to the same post are the first to receive them. They follow him with their eyes, chewing slowly. The owner of the boarding house, one Madame Valerian, does not seem interested in René, gracing him with barely a glance.

'The rest of the guests will return at night,' she says to Pierre, 'after the last prayers.' Anyway, the preceptor already knows of his arrival, and René will report to him before classes resume.

In the room there are five beds. At their feet lie trunks of different sizes that serve as tables. There are wicker baskets full of pots and clothes and two small desks. There is a square window overlooking the garden.

Pierre directs him to his trunk, taking out his uniform, books and other possessions. Without a word, he arranges everything on the bed: cutlery, a glass, pens, little bottles of ink. René will be wearing a blue silk blouse with huge puffed-sleeves and white pants with pompoms.

Pierre shows him the books. *Letters of Cicero. The Life of Saint Ignatius. Georgics of Virgil.* René does not remember the others.

'You must rest and then wash,' Pierre says. 'Your tutor will arrive before dinner, then your roommates will come back, and you will have to introduce yourself.'

René nods almost without listening. He looks at his things and tries to familiarise himself with them, to think of them as his own, but the more he stares, the stranger they become.

'We met at the Cour des Classes. Do you remember?'

'Of course. Your call was like the roar of a beast. Hic, pater! Hic, pater! Lévesque introduced you as Louis François Rêver, Mechanicus—my rhetoric and grammar partner. A simple craftsman, an apprentice blacksmith, whose hands have suffered the scold of injuries and overwork from an early age. The clothes did not fit you. The sleeves hung loose from your arms and your pants were too tight. Remember?'

'Yes. At a certain age one, can glean in a child's eyes the future course of his life. That is what I glimpsed in you. I saw in your eyes who I see now.'

On the first day of school, his heart gallops like a steed escaping from the Devil himself. His clothes are uncomfortable, and the silk rubs unpleasantly on his buttocks and arms.

He arrives at the square. He does not remember how. He must have ambled like a sleepwalker, absorbed in his daydreams. The angular arch of the entrance, with its fearsome stone façade, is like the mouth of a disguised giant that gobbles up the students. He follows the others, letting himself go.

He is in a crowded quadrangle. The faces blur around him, a throng of young people dressed identically in blue shirts and white pants. Scattered around the quad, the Fathers order the students into groups. René would not have been able to get to class that morning had it not been for Father Lévesque's intervention.

> 'We had many preceptors. I no longer remember them all, but I recall Father Lévesque with much affection. He took care of me during the first year of classes.'
>
> 'He was not actually a Father, but a student dressed like us. He was in his second year of theology at the time.'
>
> 'However, in our eyes he was always a Father.'
>
> 'You have never had such a close and trusting relationship with men as you did with the Fathers. You, who grew up surrounded by women. Then other men would come: Beeckman, Reneri, Van Zurck, Balzac, Bannius, Villebressieux.'
>
> 'Friendship is the greatest good to which we can aspire. Genuine friends are united by a bond similar to love, except that it is a type of affection that does not yearn for possession of its object.'
>
> 'A pure love, whose highest expression is the love of a father for his children, just as God loves us, his offspring.'

Father Lévesque arrives. He speaks in a slow, melodious Latin.

'Renatus, the Rector will welcome you this afternoon. Do not be afraid. You will like school. Here there are no rich or poor, no knights, peasants or kings, only men created equal in God's image.'

He leads René by the arm to his group and kneels beside him during mass. Prayer calms René's soul. He knows that God is still there and that He has not abandoned him. So begins his new life.

Seen from above, with the eyes of an angel, his days follow the same course. Like the journey of the soul, mornings begin in darkness. The preceptor lights the lamps, waking them at five.

'Excito sursum! Excito sursum!'

The preceptor taps a tin basin gently, then loudly if they are slow to rise. Invariably, René trails behind the others. He has the worst bed of all because he was the last to arrive. The ropes are loose, and the feathers slide off the mattress, sticking up his nose or to his nightgown, causing his fellows a lot of laughter.

The maid brings a vase full of water and distributes it among the pots. René takes a few sips before washing his hands and face. The first few hours of awareness are difficult due to fatigue and his congenital weakness.

The first act of the day is prayer.

'As the light of day touches his eyes, Lord, his heart lifts up to You in search of Your gaze. Listen to the words of those who feel life once more, and be attentive, Lord. Close to his open hand, give him an answer to his question. Help him in his restlessness, you, who are his Lord, in Whom I trust.'

Often, René stays dreaming behind open eyes. The creatures and places of his sleep escape from his head and continue to exist. Everything seems strange to him, and he does not recognise his companions or the Father.

Over time, he manages to overcome fear, teaching his body to obey because reason must be the shepherd of the imagination, guiding it according to its precepts and purposes. He dresses with his eyes closed and learns to kneel beside the bed without tripping over anything.

In the cold months, they go to the kitchen and dress by the fire. For breakfast they are served warm soup, bread, cheese and leftovers from the previous day. They are given meat three times a week in winter and pears and apples in the spring. As the light rises over the world, things and people regain their ordinary veneer.

These recollections bring a sour, dry taste to his mouth, one of the first sensations he has on awakening. He smells the lamps and the farts that his fellows let out during their tasks. They snicker at each other and glance at him. René thinks they do it just to torment him.

The pension is one of the last stone houses on the street that borders the river, five blocks from the central square and the entrance to the Collège. When it is winter and they go out in complete darkness, they must make an orderly line and follow the preceptor at a constant pace.

They collect stones to drive away the dogs. René prays that he won't stumble in a filthy puddle or slip in the mud, but it happens from time to time.

Dinner is served in the school dining room at six in the afternoon, then they go to their respective tutors and repeat the lessons out loud. At nine in the evening, they go to mass and return to the pension, exhausted, to say their prayers and fall into a bottomless sleep.

In the classrooms, there are a hundred students. They are his first audience, perhaps the most difficult of all the ones he will face in his life. None of his audiences will be easy.

The desks seem too high. René climbs onto the edge of the bench with difficulty and his feet dangle one step off the ground. From behind the edge of the desk, he glimpses the Father reading the day's lesson. They divide into groups of ten, each with its own decurio, to repeat the lesson. They imitate the style of the authors in their compositions.

The Latin teacher calls René to read in front of the class, then sends him back to his desk. He orders him to rise again and walk to the front. René repeats the ritual eight times until the Father is satisfied that he is doing it correctly, upright, at a moderate pace, simulating serenity and confidence.

'We learned how to address the teachers and the other students. We learned to sit, walk, dance. Your health and appearance improved noticeably. Your face took on an exuberant pink colour. It must have been the result of horse-riding, dancing and fencing. At least that is what everyone said when you went to visit your father's house. Your fragile, faltering voice soon took on fire and substance. Here, your face, that naked face that identifies you before the world and before God, was transformed into a mask. We shared three years of grammar, rhetoric, oratory and poetics. Then came the years of physics, mathematics, moral philosophy and metaphysics. I will treasure those fierce debates forever in my memory. How many times have we faced each other?'

'We discussed the nature of comets, the place of evil in God's plan, the angelic origin of the alphabet, the discovery of the moons of Jupiter, and who could forget your presentation on Seneca? What an impression you made! Our decurio, Father Nöel, prepared me for my first Saturday debates. He read my compositions and shook his head slightly, his lips pursed. I was not sure if he was trying to laugh or hide his disappointment. He wrote most of the text for my first dissertation. Of course, when it was my turn to respond to my opposant, I was left on my own.'

'A good disputatio is like a fencing match, don't you think? If you manage a successful first attack, you have already won half the fight. You were an incomparable swordsman, Renatus, and we soon saw other talents arise in you. You became an expert in deciphering the emblems of the Jesuits and came up with your own. Some of your emblems even had the honour of adorning the columns during the ceremony of the anniversary of the death of our Christian King, Henry IV, quid gloriam habet. Although you must confess that you have always been a lousy draftsman. And now that I think about it, your poetic compositions were pretty clumsy too!'

'I was not an exemplary student.'

'Your efforts were reflected in the evaluations that the Fathers kept. Here, I have them. Mores, bonus. Frequentia, assiduus. And ingenium? Let's see. Year 1608: ingenium, minus promptum; 1609: ingenium, mediocre. Oh, look what we have here! Year 1610: ingenium, perspicacissimo.'

Elemental geometry makes quite an impression on René. He learns how to build complex figures from simple elements, like lines and sections of circles. He learns how to calculate the proportions between figures and understand any type of relationship between their elements. No matter how complicated a problem is, he can break it down into its simplest parts and reassemble it according to precise directives.

He is very lonely. He even misses Pierre after his graduation. At the end of his junior year, they procure him a private room in a small, austere place in a boarding house closer to the square. He is comfortable there at night, with his thoughts. In fact, his worst moments of loneliness occur in the middle of the crowd, in classrooms, at mass and at ceremonies.

On vacation, he takes the opportunity to sleep until mid-afternoon. The bright light of day wakes him up. His father now considers him a man and is very nice to him, but René feels like he is talking to someone else, to an idea inside his head of what he wants him to be. Father insists on taking René riding and hunting in the woods. He is not a successful hunter, and the long walks in the countryside bore him.

He does not get along with his stepmother or half-brother. He enjoys spiritual retreats more than vacations, where he can be alone at last, in the company of his thoughts, fighting against his own shadow with an imaginary sword, a swordsman in the service of the King, ridding the world of Muslims, atheists, heretics and conspirators!

'Do you remember our staging of Orpheus? The theatre was the fundamental tool of our education. For the Jesuits, the art of the theatre assists in the cultivation of memory and the development of character and sensitivity.'

'I especially remember that classmate of ours. You disguised him as Eurydice. Guillaume Avenet, his name was—why do I remember that name? He was in our Fraternity of the Virgin, the one who cried all the time during our exercises. What a sweet, feminine voice!'

'The Fathers would not have allowed a woman on stage. I even considered you for the role! But the performers were responsible for their own wardrobe. Avenet was a duke's son and part of the procession that escorted the heart of our dear dead King to the school chapel. As I assumed, Avenet spared no expense on clothes and makeup. And our fellows plagued you enough because of your femininity.

So, humble squire, it was your lot to be one of the shepherds. You know, when I saw him enter the scene, I had the certainty that I was seeing the real Guillaume. Since then, off stage I would always see an impostor, an actor playing a role that did not befit him.'

'And then you had to show off with your gadgets!'

'The work needed a dénouement, a deus ex machina. The automaton was one of my first experiments. When Orpheus enters Hades in search of Eurydice, he thinks he is recovering his beloved, but he is really chasing an illusion, a spectre. And the automaton represented the transformation of Eurydice, her purification in the depths, but also her quality as ghost, the universal nature of all artifice. Orpheus's fantasy has been transmuted into a material creature. The machine had to utter six lines in Act Four. I made her move her lips while Avenet sang the verse from a hidden place, remember? We even put Avenet's clothes and wig on her.'

'The libretto had an incoherent ending that does not agree with Ovid's version nor Virgil's. I prefer Plato's in which Orpheus is punished for his lack of courage. In your version,

Orpheus is raised to heaven by the hand of Apollo himself—all just to boast about your machines and stage gadgets!'

'Orpheus's ascension to heaven was a reference to the rise of our glorious Christian King Henry IV by the hand of Jupiter and Saturn. The symbolism of his blue cape, with the fleur-de-lys embroidered in gold thread, was quite self-evident, but remember that not all the public was cultured. There were merchants and townspeople there.'

'Night is falling. It's about time you stopped intruding on my thoughts. Soon your creature will awaken and claim my attention. We must be cautious.'

'But we have not finished with the Jesuits, your teachers who would later be your judges and your allies in spreading your philosophy. Art brings to perfection that which originates in nature. Thus, the hands of the Jesuits would mould the shapeless clay of your soul. Reason is like a tenuous flame in the soul of men, a light that must be stoked with the proper practices and meditations.'

'How strange it is to hear you say something true, something clear and bright!'

'Cicero already teaches us this. Reason must impose on nature its own forms and designs, which are like shadows of the divine plan. Natura machinata. The design of the Collège already manifests this idea in the symmetrical arrangement of its classrooms and quadrangles, in the geometry of its gardens, in the strict organisation of hours and activities, and in the structure of reasoning: inventio, dispositio, elocutio, memory, exercitatio, imitatio.'

'Your thoughts seem to be echoes of mine.'

'Or maybe yours are shadows of mine?'

'A ghastly possibility! And clearly absurd. Do you hear that? She is waking up.'

'Our work of devotion, Renatus! It's a pity that we will not get to hear the story of the end of your childhood. It all started with the return of the fevers, didn't it? The awakening of your body was a painful event that manifested itself for the first time in the depth of your dreams. Shapeless dreams punctuated by judders that shook your body. You would faint during morning classes and be excused from attending the ten o'clock mass. Your father had to intercede and go directly to the Rector, Father Charlet, a distant relative of yours. For a while they let you get up late and take the morning classes in your room with Dinet.'

'Again, your thoughts confuse themselves with mine. But the lamps have already gone out, leaving us with the icy glow of this full moon. It has been a long day, and I think it is time you left me alone. Except I am afraid to enter my dreams, knowing that you will be there too.'

'Let me lull you to sleep, then. Is this not perhaps the most appropriate time to invoke Orpheus himself? Because the girl is our spectre, our artifice against death.'

'Do what you like. You may be very skilled in oratory and the mechanical arts, although you are nothing but a sophist. I am no longer listening to you.'

Have you died, my life, and I still breathe?
You have left my side
never to return and I remain here?
No! If there is any virtue left in my song,
I will go to the deepest abyss
and soften the heart of the king of shadows
and bring you back to see the stars;
Or, if impious destiny denies me this,
I shall stay with you, in the company of death.
Goodbye, earth; goodbye, sky and sun; goodbye.

8

In which strange dreams are shown, prompting young Descartes on his way to the Truth, and where, to the great delight and instruction of the reader, some Cartesian notions are presented regarding perception and the nature of ideas.

Although the distribution of the stars appears irregular throughout the various parts of the universe, I have no doubt that there is a natural order between them that is regular and determinate. Grasping this order is the key and the foundation of the highest and perfect science of material things that men will ever achieve, because its possession would allow us to discover a priori all the different forms and essences of terrestrial bodies, which otherwise we could only guess after the fact and from their effects.

—René Descartes

'Oh father, there you are again. And who is that man with such a serious expression? He seems to be putting my father through an exam.'

'That man is Johann Faulhaber, celebrated mathematician and alchemist, member of the Rosicrucian Order, and whom we might consider your father's second great teacher. Faulhaber does not speak French, Dutch or Latin, and our hero does not speak a word of German, but they both understand the universal language of numbers and figures.'

'And what is *this?*'

'I'm still not satisfied with these tableaux. It is difficult to establish an adequate balance between mimesis and the formal requirements of the work. In this case we have divided the tableaux into four parts with the intention of presenting the audience with a strange coincidence of dates. Come, I will show you quickly.

'Here, on the right, we begin with November 10, 1616, the day your father obtained his degree and license in Civil Law from the University of Poitiers.

'In the adjacent scene, we witness the first meeting between Descartes and his first teacher, the engineer and mathematician Isaac Beeckman, which took place on November 10, 1618, exactly two years later. The two men became close friends, and Beeckman had a decisive influence on Descartes's thought.

'Here, on the night of November 10, 1619, as we shall see very soon, Descartes had a series of dreams in which his life's destiny was revealed to him. Given the importance of this event, we have included it in the work.

'And finally, a year later, on November 10, 1620, while wandering the city of Prague after the overthrow of Frederick V, Descartes wrote in his notebook that he had begun to envision the foundation of a portentous discovery. This was shortly after his encounter with the great astronomer and mathematician Johannes Kepler.'

'What a curious coincidence, it's true! I wonder what it could mean.'

'I am not satisfied with the painting in the background. It's difficult to represent a city as beautiful and mysterious as Prague, a city of conspiracies, gardens, alleys and whispers.'

'It's a magnificent job! I wish one day to visit these beautiful places, or maybe it should be enough for me to walk through your fictional streets and lose myself in your stunningly lifelike paintings.'

'I am very grateful, damoiselle. Let us see. Here we have Paris, Breda, Copenhagen, Amsterdam, Danzig, Frankfurt, Neuburg, Rome, Prague and Breslaw. And beyond, the roads and landscapes of Denmark, Holland, Poland, Hungary, Italy, Germany, Bohemia and Brittany. Our hero enlisted in various armies and for more than ten years travelled these places, seeking to learn from the book of the world.'

'My father took me to Paris, but I didn't see anything because he left me in the trunk. I do not want to go back to that trunk.'

'Paris, you see, was a great party. Your father was very good at playing cards. Here we see him betting—and there he is also, wandering through the salons and dazzling with his mathematical skills. Here we see the Hôtel de Bourgogne and the Théâtre du Marais, the two Parisian theatres that your father frequented. The social life of Paris is vain and superficial, and this leads your father to many disappointments. Visitors come to pester him at all hours of the day, and he begins to yearn for solitude. People, to tell the truth, find him somewhat arrogant, ambitious and bombastic. However, your father manages to establish intimate relationships with prestigious and wealthy scientists and scholars. Well, we have arrived.'

'The next Act?'

'And here come the chimes. Just in time! You must take shelter. Fate does not always choose pleasant days.'

This time it is she who starts the march towards the foot of the stage, where the steps await, ascending into the darkness. It is the darkness of a cold and cruel night skewered by winds that ram against the roofs and windows.

'Let us hurry, before your mechanisms are ruined in this dire weather.'

It is the eve of Saint Martin's Day. The wheat has been harvested, tomorrow the pigs and geese will be slaughtered, and the peasants will gather at the city gates to await the distribution of the wine. The town seems empty now, but in the houses the party will continue until late. If you listen carefully, the wind will bring you a shred of laughter, a bit of music or the clink of pots hitting the floor. Amid all this, the wise river, which once marked the limit of the Roman Empire, remains oblivious to the storm. The rain barely stings de la Vega's grey and luminescent countenance, apparently forged from the same stone that makes up the buildings on its margins.

'Francine, see that white building that takes up an entire corner? The residence belongs to a local merchant, an educated man and lover of mathematics. See that light in the window, the only one visible on the entire façade? That is where we are headed. I warn you that we will get wet, but soon we will be back in that warm room, remember? It is good there, an ideal place to meditate. It will be a well-deserved rest for us.

'Let us now enjoy the fact that we are able to expose ourselves and wander the streets like mere mortals. If someone happens to spot our figures, they will surely judge that we are a mirage, mere disturbances of light in the agitated air. Après vous, Francine. We will enter through the main door. The room is behind the second door on your right. We will go, with your permission, my princess. We will be unnoticed. The philosopher is very immersed in his thoughts. Take this opportunity to warm up next to the stove.'

The heat is hellish compared to the cold they have come from. It is a modest room, with wooden walls and a plaster ceiling. There is a cot and a desk with various objects: a tin bowl with traces of dirty water, a razor, a mirror and a comb. The iron stove takes up a leading place, embedded in the wall of the room. A telescope can be seen, mounted on a tripod. It is an instrument built by Polybius, the pseudonym young Descartes has chosen. It does not work very well, but the chromatic aberrations have awoken his interest.

On the desk are two neatly lined sheaves of papers: a stack of blank sheets and a smaller stack of scrawled sheets. There is an inkwell, a wooden pot, an hourglass, a pen, a leather briefcase and three books: the Bible, *On Wisdom* by Pierre Charron, and *De occulta philosophia* by Cornelius Agrippa. The latter is a loan from Hypolite, an Earl of Bretagne and companion in the army.

The Count treats Polybius with the stylised deference that nobles use to address the lower classes. Although Polybius is a man of the law, to them he is a mere squire, the son of a member of Parliament. Hypolite, on the other hand, belongs to the nobility, and next spring he will return to his lands to inherit titles and fortunes. Polybius will continue to travel the world, seeking the kind of wealth that no amount of gold can buy—the spiritual wealth that flows from true knowledge. To seal this resolution, next summer he plans to go on a pilgrimage to the Sanctuary of Our Lady of Loreto.

Polybius is standing. He is a small and scrawny man, with a soft, pale and mercurial face. His hair is long and dry, of a dark brown colour. He has a week-old beard, but his chin and the fine moustache bordering his upper lip can still be seen. He wears a clean but wrinkled white shirt that reaches his knees, baggy canvas trousers, silk stockings and leather slippers with wooden soles. The fingers of his left hand manipulate a small piece of wax that softens as his fingers infuse it with heat. The habit of shaping wax calms his tremors and helps him think.

Where will fate take me? What is my purpose in this life?

Since he enlisted and arrived here with the troops, an infantry belonging to Duke Maximilian of Bavaria, Polybius has spent most of his time in this room. He takes his daily walks through the empty alleys, visits the bookstores and enjoys wonderful evenings with Faulhaber. But the truth is, he is not in good spirits. He sleeps too much and has returned to his habit of staying in bed late. A servant brings him a meal in the morning, a light breakfast of milk, bread and fruits. He eats his lunch in the kitchen with the servants, in silence.

Today the food has been abundant, especially the meat, but Polybius eats moderately and refuses the wine. Wine drives away the Muses and the digestion of the meat slows down his already fragile humours. Only the cannabis can clear his spirits.

Polybius takes *De occulta philosophia* from the table. The journey has been arduous and strewn with pitfalls. He is determined to learn from the book of the world, but so far he has learned that the world writes in tangled, blood-smeared sentences. Before leaving on his travels, Polybius believed that the journey would not bring great complications. He believed that, in his role as gentilhomme de l'artillerie, he would not run into conflict or bloodshed. It is true that he has witnessed only one battle, and from a more than prudent distance; however, the bloody wars have left their mark everywhere throughout the continent.

More than a book, the world is a stream of signs scattered in the wind. War rages everywhere and the old order crumbles. The world is cast into uncertainty, shattered in the clash of political ambitions and frivolous theological discrepancies. A fresh corpse always attracts insects, and he has seen them come out of hiding, buzzing in his ears, spreading their colourful wings. Invisible sects, charlatans, preachers and secret societies flourish in the cracks. Astrologers, magicians, soothsayers, alchemists and vainglorious sages swarm everywhere, all claiming to have discovered the key to the eternal and immutable Truth.

Yet amid the tumult and confusion, a new order sparkles in the ashes. Polybius has conversed with astronomers, philosophers, mathematicians, alchemists, theologians, craftsmen and architects. He has conferred with hermetists from Bohemia, engineers from Holland and lens polishers from Italy. He has wandered through innumerable theatres and salons where all kinds of new theories and speculations are woven. Although no one paid much attention to him (why should they?), he has listened and learned.

How many are the existing elements that make up the composition of natural things? What is the effect of heat? What is the earth, what is the air and what do they produce?

What is the origin of the heavens? What is the cause of the ebb of the sea and the rainbow of various colours? What gives clouds the power to excite loud thunder? Where does lightning come from?

What is the secret cause that makes us see meteorites and comets? What is the hidden power that makes the earth tremble? Where do the gold and iron mines come from? Where does the secret virtue of nature come from?

Agrippa is promptly left on the desk. Polybius approaches the stove and is absorbed in the task of lighting a clay pipe. He likes to watch the flames of the lamp. He can do it for hours. Light, that body without matter that is like a pure idea.

His short fingers bring a twig to the flame. He lights the pipe, and the pungent, sweet aroma of marijuana spreads through the air. He inhales hard and studies the fading smoke trails. He glimpses a fleeting movement in the window. Maybe it is the housekeeper bringing firewood to the stove on the other side of the wall. Sometimes the lady wanders slowly and late in the hallways and around the house. Unfortunately, the woman speaks French and takes advantage of any pretext, such as bringing food or communicating a message from the owner, to engage him in endless conversations. No, it must be just the wind. And the rain.

Moreover, he has forgotten about the storm, so engrossed has he been in his meditations. Now he hears the wind and rain banging on windows and pecking at the roof. He sucks on the pipe, blows the smoke from his nose and resumes the inner dialogue. On this occasion, his interlocutor is Diophantes and, more than a dialogue, it is a soliloquy.

If you had entrusted the method to posterity, instead of showing only its results, we would have the Science of Sciences in our power.

On the walls, Polybius's shadow looms over his hunched body. The heat stirs the air, and his shadow seems to be on fire. He turns heavily on his heels and heads for the cot.

I can solve all your problems: the square as the sum of two squares. Add the same number to two given numbers to get two squares. After all, your problems are like your machines: mere tricks to impress ignorant crowds.

He sits on the cot and falls to one side. Polybius normally sleeps naked, but he has no intention of sleeping.

With my compasses I have taken the first accurate steps towards a new foundation of knowledge. I will begin by showing you my solution to the problem of trisecting an angle.

His eyes close, his hand still holding the pipe. In Paris, when servants knocked, he pretended to be asleep.

All truths must be built on the foundation of a single and unquestionable Truth.

However, when he achieves that longed-for loneliness, the ideas proliferate, disperse and do not let themselves be caught, like a flock of birds or a collapsing construction built on faulty ground. Is there an art of dreams? A Lullian art?

Who is there? No, it is not the housekeeper. His gaze is fixed on the darkness until he sees the two shadows. *What a pretty girl. As beautiful as Truth itself!*

They trudge on the soft and slippery ground. The narrow passageways inside the philosopher's brain are made of folds and bumps, and all the surfaces are covered with small pores that alternate between emitting and inhaling jets of ethereal, agitated vapour. The openings are the mouths of tubes that lead to the various parts of the body, carrying sensations and causing the movements of the living machine. It is hotter here than in the room!

De la Vega indicates the small holes with a flowery gesture.

'Here we can verify that ancient conceptions about life are false. There are no immaterial souls in nature and no mysterious agencies causing the movements of living bodies. Life is, like the world, nothing more than matter operating according to the laws of mechanics.'

The spirits are agitated. The dense brain network shudders to the rhythm of discharges and aspirations. De la Vega waves his arms to disperse the effusions of the pores. The aroma is sour and intoxicating, with a hint of sulphur and cloves.

'The patterns formed on these surfaces are the corporeal ideas. Here we see a childhood memory. And that man with the thin beard and lively eyes is Beeckman. There, the shower of sparks is a reminder of the fireworks during Ferdinando II's coronation in Frankfurt two months ago.'

'And what is that thing there in the centre?'

'Oh, that is a very special gland called the conarium. It is the organ that connects the body with the immortal soul, the source of thinking and the will. See those little holes? The shapes that appear there are transmitted to the immaterial mind. The soul responds, altering the movements and exhalations of the spirits, thus allowing us to exercise our dominion over the body and over the world.'

'It looks like a cabbage. So, can I see the soul from here?'

'I'm afraid it's not possible, my dear. But I promise you that we will see something even more edifying. Follow me over here. Be careful, it's very dark.'

Polybius falls asleep on his left side in an uncomfortable position, like a puppet abandoned in a hurry. His idea—the idea of Polybius—walks aimlessly through the corridors of his brain, leaning towards his left. His right hand remains in the same awkward position as in the real world: wrist bent, palm up, thumb sticking to the side. The breath of the spirits has been transformed into a terrible wind that lashes the dreamer with great fury, as if it wanted to sweep him back into the world.

The dreamer finds himself wandering down a street. The town is pretty and orderly, with wide streets and tall grey stone façades. It reminds him of Châtellerault. Polybius senses diffuse and fearsome presences that observe him.

The wind rages and pushes him. Polybius loses his balance and begins to spin like a top. He manages to regain his stability, although his body is still hunched over. Looking up, he notices a church in the middle distance. It is a small construction located on the edge of a large central courtyard. In truth, now that he can see better, it is more of a chapel that could belong to a school or barracks. Whatever it is, the place promises to be a refuge.

With great difficulty, he makes his way there. He will pray with great devotion, asking God to free him from the infernal creatures that haunt him. As he crosses the threshold of the chapel, he notices, in the corner of his eye, a shadow passing in the opposite direction. He discovers that from the inside the place looks like a cathedral more than a chapel. The vaults, stairs and corridors multiply without end. At the end of the central aisle, the distant altar is barely visible.

'Bonsoir, Sieur Duperron,' greets the shadow. It must be someone he knows. But he wants to be alone, to dedicate himself to his studies, his great and important work.

Now he remembers who it is!

Of course, that is Monsieur M. What is he doing here? Shouldn't he be in Paris? Am I in Paris? How careless. I have not returned the greeting. What will he think of me!

He turns around and runs but progress is slow. With effort, he manages to leave the place. The courtyard is completely deserted. Polybius cannot spot his acquaintance. He then realises that he has not prayed. He has turned his back on God!

At that moment, a powerful gust of wind drags him aside until he is cornered against an external wall of the chapel. From there, Polybius spots a shadowy figure in the courtyard. Despite the wind, he can clearly hear the stranger's words as if he were speaking in his ear.

'Sieur Duperron, what a pleasant surprise! How are you? I see that you have risen early today and that you have come to offer your prayers like a devout Christian.'

Polybius is in the middle of the courtyard. He does not remember walking that far and keeps leaning to the left because of this ridiculous cramp that prevents him from standing erect.

The stranger smiles at him. Now Polybius can see him clearly: a tall, somewhat stooped fellow with broad shoulders and of indefinite age. His features are very marked, almost exaggerated: large dark eyes, an eagle's nose, wide ears. The terrible wind does not seem to affect him, and his hair and cape remain motionless.

The stranger speaks.

'Have you seen Monsieur S.? If you could be so kind, I have something to give him. Perhaps you know where he is. Perhaps you would be so kind as to deliver this to him.'

An object materialises in the stranger's hands. Polybius is taken aback at the thick and misshapen fingers, like old roots. The man is holding a huge egg that comes from a distant land, perhaps from the Americas or Africa. It occurs to Polybius that at any moment the egg will give birth to an extraordinary chimera, but now that he can see it better, it resembles fruit, with a soft, textured skin like velvet. It is a melon, Polybius decides. A melon pregnant with seeds.

A group of people surround the stranger. They may have been there all along, following the conversation. Polybius shudders to think that the demons have returned, but these people are flesh and blood, dressed in Parisian fashion, laden in shiny silk and feathered hats. Their faces are hard to see, their features constantly changing like projections on smoke screens. There is also a young woman, hardly more than a girl, to the right of the stranger. Her face is familiar.

Again, that discomfort, that guilt, as if he were naked in the middle of the crowd. They are laughing at him, as they laughed at him in Paris.

Suddenly the strangers disappear, and the idea of Polybius finds itself alone, again, in the courtyard.

De la Vega and Francine return to the room.

'Have we already left the dream?'

'Maybe all life is a dream!'

'Then someone must be dreaming it.'

Polybius is lying on the bed, in the same position as they left him.

'It's true! We can concoct the most splendorous or frightening dreams, but we can never dream the dreamer. Go now, my empress. Let us hide before the sleeper awakens!'

Before retiring to his place behind the stove, de la Vega administers a good tap on the sleeper's ribs. Polybius fidgets on the cot and opens his eyes.

'Mon dieu.'

His gaze searches the room. What a relief! It was all just a dream. He is glad. He tentatively massages his ribs and gazes at his hands until he is fully convinced that he is awake. He changes his position and lies on his right side, facing the wall. This calms the pain a bit.

A melon. Could it be the philosopher's stone?

He feels too weak to arise, but his mind is strangely clear and awake.

A demon is trying to captivate me. This wall, these hands, this pain—maybe they are not the same as a moment ago.

No, he must not succumb to doubt, to the demons of the dream. He recites a prayer to himself.

Oh, good Jesus, hear me. Within your wounds, hide me.

The wind undoubtedly represents the forces of evil that want to divert him from the right path.

Do not let me draw away from You.

There are no demons.

Nature is only matter.

From the evil enemy, defend me. At the hour of my death, call me.

He remains in that position for a long time, meditating on the evils and suffering of the world. Without realising it, he falls asleep. Again, the idea of Polybius prowls the fuzzy corridors of an undefined dream.

He hears distant voices. There is a formidable noise, like thunder, and the dreamer wakes with a start. His body flips over, heavily. He sways on the edge of the cot for a moment. He sits up and looks around the room. A shower of luminous points flutters in the air like the sparks of a wildfire. His eyes can't focus on objects in the room. The spectacle captivates him. He stays there, staring at the little lights until they fade.

Lights, seeds. Where has he seen seeds?

Are these lights the seeds of wisdom that sleep in the soul of all men?

Then Polybius notices something out of place. He sits up and goes to the desk.

His books are missing—who has stolen them? His papers and writing implements have also disappeared. A bulky and heavy book takes their place. Without thinking, he opens it and discovers that it is a dictionnaire universel.

This may be useful to me. He thumbs through the contents. *Débâcler, débarasser, geleur, géline, gélinotte.*

He sees that another book, thin and small, has appeared by the side of the encyclopaedia. Polybius rushes to find the title. It is the *Corpus omnium veterum poetarum latinorum*, an anthology of ancient authors.

When he opens it at random, the first sentence he sees is 'Quod vital sectabor iter?'

What path in life am I to follow?

He continues to read.

'The courts are full of uproar; our home overwhelmed by worries; the problems in our home follow us when we travel; the merchant always has new losses to fear, and the fear of the vilest poverty does not let him rest; the farmer is exhausted from his work; for the sailor, the horrendous shipwreck lends the ocean an ominous name.'

He receives the nagging feeling that he is not alone.

'What are you doing here?'

'It occurred to me that you might be interested in reading this too,' says the tall, well-dressed man with the long, curled hair. A hand with thick, crooked fingers holds out a handwritten sheet of paper. 'It is an excellent composition.'

Polybius hesitates a moment, then takes the paper.

'Yes, I know this poem. It's one of the Idylls of Ausonius. I can recite it from memory: "Yes and no: everyone constantly uses these familiar monosyllables. If you take them out, you will leave nothing for men's tongues to argue with. In them everything is found, and everything is in them; whether it's a matter of business or pleasure, of bustle or rest." A copy of the poem is in this anthology. I know the book very well.'

'Where did you get the anthology?'

'Someone left it on the table. We studied it with the Jesuits. It's very strange. I do not remember. I had three books here that later disappeared. There was an encyclopaedia and now there is nothing.'

'What do you say? Here it is! It hasn't gone anywhere.'

It is true. The encyclopaedia has reappeared on the table. Polybius opens it and realises that it is incomplete. Entire sections are missing. For example, it jumps from *H* to *K*. As he turns the pages, the book changes before his eyes. He can't find the same page twice. It is an infinite book and at the same time eternally incomplete.

He puts it on the table and takes the smaller one.

'Let me find you the poem. How strange. Where is it? Anyway, I know of a better poem, also by Ausonio, which begins "Quod vitae sectabor iter…".'

The gentleman's face is covered in shadow. It is hard to guess his expression. 'Show me, please.'

But the book has changed again. The pages show a series of engravings, detailed portraits executed with an exquisite, almost otherworldly naturalism. Although he can't identify the people in the portraits, he has never seen images so faithful to reality.

'This book is very beautiful, I have never seen anything like it, but it's not the book we had at La Flèche.'

The nobleman raises his hands as a preacher might.

'Yes and no, being and not-being. It's an old problem, perhaps the central problem of philosophy.'

'Arguably, yes. It's the problem of all men: the choice between two paths in life. Being is perfection, good, unity and justice. Non-being is evil, deception, the void.'

And with these words Polybius finds himself awake, sprawled on the cot.

The first thing he does is look at the desk. The three books are there just as he left them. Regardless, he is wary of taking this as a definite indication that he is awake. He rushes to the desk and inspects the pages, squeezing the paper between his fingertips. He carefully studies everything around him, including the shadows and the light from the lamp. The certainty that he is indeed awake takes a long time to settle in.

In any case, he should not waste this moment of inspiration. Polybius hurriedly uncaps the ink, spilling droplets onto his fingers and the papers. He takes the piece of wax in his left hand and squeezes it with all his might as his other hand begins to write.

By this time, the visitors have left.

9

Where a murky event is revealed concerning the posthumous writings of the great philosopher.

'Hear that applause, Francine? It's for you.'

'I can't see anyone.'

'In this next Act, you will have a chance to rest.'

'How long before I have to appear next?'

'Calm and patience! You must be born first, then…'

'Come on, say it. *Die.*'

'Only to be born again! My Francine, you have the leading role in the play, and it has cost me a lot of effort to ensure your immortality. After your father's death, his letters and unpublished manuscripts fell into the hands of certain men concerned with sanctifying him and bequeathing to posterity the image of a pious, orthodox and Catholic philosopher. They erased anything that could ruin that image. Even you and your mother! I saved what I could.'

The course of their feet leads them through another area lit under hanging lamps. In the centre of the disc of light, a stream of smoke rises toward the distant ceiling. There is a small fire there—a real fire this time. A large, open trunk lies near the fire and shadows are visible around it. As they approach, Francine counts four human silhouettes.

Something stirs in the air. She thinks it is moths, but then she discovers pieces of paper drifting slowly from the heights to form a layer of ash on the ground. Some of the pieces are still on fire, others are brittle embers.

Francine ignores the courteous pull from Don de la Vega, who urges her to continue.

'But it's you!'

The Señor gives up. 'Pardon?'

'That man on the left is you! I mean, an actor who looks a lot like you. You even wear the same clothes. Amazing! What is all this? And who are those other three men?'

'Their names won't mean much to you, but if you really want to know, they are Claude Clerselier, Jean de Raeyand and Cornelis van Hogelande.'

The girl picks up a burnt piece of paper.

'And this? It contains symbols that are still legible.'

'It is written in a secret code. It contains a very special discovery concerning solids. More precisely, the proportion between the faces, vertices and edges of any three-dimensional polyhedron. The sum of the number of faces and vertices minus the number of edges always equals two.'

Francine is not paying attention. With a little jump, she snatches a piece of paper from the air and reads aloud.

'...no more than two hours weaving. Work is good for her because it exercises her hands and her senses, but the girl is too young to work.'

Reluctantly, de la Vega joins the game. He snatches a floating piece at random and recites.

'...the tubes show truly amazing craftsmanship. I have found some problems with the magnifying glass, especially the depth of field, which is very narrow and loses focus easily...'

It is Francine's turn. 'As I told you, money is no problem. In fact, together with this letter, I entrust Monsieur P. with a small gift of...'

'...it will not give you problems. You need to rest as much as possible. Do not perform tasks that require bending over or sitting on your knees for long periods of time. If the weight makes you uncomfortable, you can take any of the pillows in the room...'

'...every day, every hour without you is pure suffering. I can't work, I can hardly concentrate on writing these accursed letters...'

'…they have been delayed with the printing of the galleys and have assured me that they will be ready this Friday. I can't wait to leave this place…'

'…the work is monotonous and exhausting, but I have finished adjusting the connections to the pores of the brain. Much remains to be done. I look forward to your next visit to check that your famous esprits artificiels are what you promise…'

'…I think I have found the perfect material for the crystalline humour of the eyes…'

'…Heaven's consolation is only for children. There are certain moments when I doubt that there is an eternal world beyond this…'

'…it is difficult to imagine an existence beyond the body. Will I be able to recognise myself, continue to be who I am? I will surely remember my life in this world; however, will that be enough?'

Overcome with emotion, Francine stops reading, and her fingers loosen. The piece of paper traces a downward spiral to the ground. Don de la Vega pulls a white handkerchief from his sleeve and rushes to help her.

He gently takes her by the arm and guides her to the next stage.

10

Where the philosopher falls in love.

The Truth is imperturbable, unlimited, colourless, without form, indivisible, naked, clear, comprehensible by itself, unchangeable, good, and totally incorporeal... Return to yourself and you will understand, desire it and so it will be. Purge the senses from the body and free yourself from the irrational afflictions of matter.

—Hermes Trismegistus

Every vortex harbours a centre of stillness. And here, he is a shadow. Look at all these people! It would be impossible to find such absolute solitude anywhere else in the world. Here, in the midst of markets and merchants, mired in the anonymous and frenzied tumult, the spirit can proclaim its full freedom. They will no longer harass him as they did in Paris, where everyone recognises him on the streets.

'There goes Descartes, the famous philosopher who has not published anything!'

'He is rather short. I imagined him taller.'

'I have heard that he has been working on his new system of the world for many years, a complete philosophy that will replace that of Aristotle himself! Everything will be explained there, from the fart of a louse to the existence of the Almighty, through the ideas that are formed in our minds and how the planets move in their orbits.'

Paris, the place of so many fears and failures. Paris, the lair of his staunch enemy Gilles de Roberval, who is now a Professor at the Collège Royal—can you believe it? Instead, here he walks each day amid the bustling crowd with the same freedom and tranquillity one would find on country walks, paying the same attention to the people around that one would pay to trees in the woods.

Here children play marbles on the cobblestones and kites fly in the sky, and the sailors' footsteps sway lightly to the beat of beer and distant waves. Here products from all corners of the earth land on the docks and spread colours and aromas in the markets. Here the noise of the carriages is deafening.

> 'This year, Francine, the City Council has banned carriages on the streets, but, as you can see, the rich merchants and the Council members themselves refuse to abide by the decree. Here we do not have the need to hide. We could have descended from any of those ships, coming from a distant land—America, Africa or the Indies. We could be Prince and Princess of the Amazon. I see you like the idea!'

It is easy to get lost. The city stands on concentric levees connected by bridges. Narrow houses line the canals with colourful façades and long windows, topped by stepped gables or in the shape of a neck or a bell.

> 'We'll stop here. This is the house. A secret passage will lead us inside.'

Two delivery men carry provisions through the side door. In the main room, Thomas Sergeant instructs one of his maids about the newly arrived tenants. Sergeant is French, a thin, stern-looking man who speaks a soft, almost inaudible Dutch that stumbles on the consonants. He is a schoolteacher and owner of a bookstore in the city.

'Monsieur Descartes is not to be disturbed for any reason except for meals. He should always have something to eat in his room: fresh fruit, water and bread.'

The girl nods but seems not to listen. Her hands rest on her front, and her body rocks slightly.

In the upper room, Renatus sits quietly, pen in hand. He watches the bustling of passers-by out the window. He has not shaved in two days, and he is still in his nightgown. After a while, the crowd has lost all traces or connotations of humanity. The smudges of capes and hats are like particles dragged in a liquid. The gaze returns to the blank page. He moulds the wax between his fingers and writes.

If I look out the window and see men crossing the square, I would normally say that I see the men themselves. But what do I see except hats and capes that could hide automata? I judge that they are men. In this way, something that I thought I saw with my eyes is, in fact, understood only with the faculty of judgment that is in my mind.

A soft knock startles him. Renatus looks at his hands, very still on the desk. Could they really be his hands? The men in the square are men again. Jean, his valet, is sleeping in bed, fully dressed, with his hat and boots.

Is it time for lunch? Is he hungry? He goes to the door reluctantly. He opens it slightly, leaving a narrow slit.

'Monsieur? Sorry for the intrusion.'

Renatus stares at the woman. Fleetingly, he saw her yesterday. She is certainly beautiful. They are about the same height and their gazes meet openly and directly. The maid's eyes are vast, transparent, of a light-blue tint. Her teeth are proportioned like pearls on a necklace. Her curly, gold-coloured hair escapes from her cap and tinkles on her full, flushed cheeks like apricots.

Her ordinary clothes detract from her. She should be a princess. In his body, the spirits stir and circulate.

Renatus feels awake, mysteriously alive.

'Are you okay, Monsieur?'

The beautiful woman has been talking to him, and it is difficult to judge how long they have been there on the threshold. In his dishevelled nightgown, he has the appearance of a homeless man recovering from a night of drunkenness. He feels ashamed, and the shame stirs his blood and speeds the march of his heart. This makes him feel even more like a silly goose.

'Yes, Madame,' he says finally. 'I feel very good.'

The girl's giggle is like the gurgling of spring water.

'This is the first time in my life that someone has called me Madame! If there is something you are not sure how to say, please feel free to speak in French. I understand quite a bit of French. See, in the houses where… Oh, but I'm pestering you! Excuse me! It's just that... Monsieur Sergeant wants to know if you are hungry and if you would like to have your lunch in the bedroom. We have fresh fish, and the master has taught me how to cook two or three sauces in the French style.'

She tilts her head to the side and waits for the tenant's response. As her gaze shifts, her left eye drifts to one side, so that each eyeball focuses on a different point on Renatus's face. As a boy, he had fallen in love with a girl with crossed eyes. The imprint that those wayward orbs had left on his brain was mixed with the feeling of love, so that the two ideas remain associated. Since then, he has been prone to love women with this defect.

'Hear that sound? Call it chance, predestination, divine intervention, Cupid or the clinamen of ancient atomism. The truth is, the hidden gears of the world—or those of our history, which is the same—have made a fatal turn. Let philosophers worry about nomenclature, precise analysis, classification and the question of origins and causes! The heart has its own ideas, which reason finds inexplicable.'

Renatus can't remember opening the door, but in fact it is open.

'We haven't been introduced yet, but I'm sure Monsieur Sergeant will do so as soon as the opportunity presents itself. My name is René, but you can call me Reyner if it's easier for you. And do not treat me like nobility. The formal address makes me uncomfortable.'

The girl's heavenly gaze brushes against the instruments, the clothes, the half-unpacked trunks.

'My name is Helena.' She bows slightly, bending her knees under her thick skirts. 'But you can call me Hélène.'

'Again, Helena, don't treat me formally, please. You make me feel old and important.'

She laughs again. Her round, pale face comes alive, taking on an angel's beauty. Renatus finds it remarkable that the smile is the reason behind the deviation of the left eye. There is a connection between the muscles.

'Tell Monsieur Sergeant we'll be down in an hour.'

As he closes the door, he realises that Jean is awake and has been watching them, reclining on the bed. Renatus returns to his desk and inverts the hourglass.

'Mon dieu!' Jean exclaims. 'There are pretty women in this country!'

'Don't blaspheme. There are also fanatical preachers here, and we must go unnoticed. Come on, finish unpacking at once. I'm hungry.'

Sometime later, shaved and dressed in his cape, hat, sword and boots, Renatus Cartesius descends the stairs and heads to the kitchen. Helena welcomes him and Renatus announces that he will have lunch there.

Helena serves the food: herring with cream and mustard sauce, accompanied by boiled carrots and turnips. She pours the monsieur a pot of fresh water and leaves the jug on the table, after which she requests permission to leave. Renatus asks her to sit with him. Surprised and somewhat frightened, the maid obeys.

Renatus chews his lunch slowly, silently. Soon after, Sergeant returns from the street with a book in his hands.

'I know you're a fan of Kepler optics. Your discourse on the structure of the eye follows the guidelines of the *Ad vitellionem*.'

'So, it does. How come you've read my treatise on optics?'

'Your ideas are well known.'

Sergeant sits across from him and shows him the book. It is the latest work of Johannes Kepler. Renatus studies the cover. His eyes sway from side to side, following the momentum of the symbols.

'*Somnium*,' he murmurs.

'*The Dream.* It came from Frankfurt yesterday. The book tells an ingenious fable about a trip to the moon. The protagonist of the story is transported there by demons. The fable is a treatise on lunar astronomy. The cleverest thing is that Kepler shows us that an inhabitant of the moon would not notice the movement of his own planet, in the same way that we do not perceive the movement of our Earth. In this way, the book is a defence of Copernicus's theory in which the sun is the true centre of the universe.'

Sergeant sends Helena to sweep the floors. Renatus hears the distant murmur coming from the street and the sound of Helena at work. The Dutch are so clean. They spend all day cleaning and washing.

He contemplates the remains of his lunch.

'I, too, have tried to present my treatise on the world under the guise of a fable, a tale about the creation of the earth and of men.'

Renatus adjusts the cape around his shoulders as if he were cold. A sour smile is outlined on his lips. He abandoned his treatise on the world after learning of Galileo's condemnation by the Inquisition. The work cost him a lot of time and effort, but his entire system of physics depends on the truth of the Copernican theory. Renatus does not want to publish anything that offends the Church, and he is seeking the support of his former teachers, the Jesuits, to spread his ideas.

'Copernicus, Kepler and Galileo have not been able to explain the nature of the forces that carry the planets in their orbits. I have shown how celestial bodies are carried in their courses by whirlpools of subtle matter, how the universe was formed by the action of these same eddies. Now I must find another way to present my ideas.'

Renatus is sorry for having talked so much. His deep *tristesse* overflows his body and sparkles through his eyes.

Sergeant breaks the silence.

'Mersenne has just published Galileo's *Mechanics* and a summary of his *Discourse* in French. I've ordered some copies. Can I tempt you with a snack? I have plum liquor and French cognac.'

'You can tempt me. I've already given up on this day. Cognac, please. As long as it's not beer. They drink it in excess around here!'

'You'll get used to it.'

'I've lived in these parts for more than six years. I don't think I'll ever get used to it.'

'I hope you find here the peace of mind you need to think and continue your work. I am outside, mostly, and my servants are as silent as mice. So, let's toast to that.'

'I sincerely thank you.'

'The old scholasticism is collapsing. No matter how hard they try to silence it, the truth of the new science will triumph over the dusty dogmatism of the Aristotelians.'

'In any case, we must proceed with caution. We must not propose new opinions but offer new arguments that preserve the old opinions, even if only in appearance and name. In this way, no one can object to our arguments, and those who understand will know very well what we are saying.'

'I see! Like the Trojan horse in which Ulysses hid his troops?'

'You can think of it that way. I'm trying to salvage everything I can from those years of work. I am preparing a discourse in which I present my new method for science. I will include treatises on optics, meteorology and geometry. That enormous effort may not have been in vain after all.'

'I see that we will have interesting after-dinner talks.'

'I have to go for a walk, otherwise I'll feel drowsy. Thank you very much for the cognac. It has brought back memories of that place that I still call home.'

'You'll be back, sometime.'

'Every time I visit France, it seems to me an increasingly strange place. I would rather share the rest of eternity with the Dutch than with my French compatriots.'

Sergeant raises his glass.

'I completely agree. There are no French in Heaven!'

The philosopher laughs out loud.

'Let's hope we're the first, then.'

During his stay in Amsterdam, Renatus continues his research in optics. He receives Beeckman, who shows him the treatise by Galileo that the Church has condemned. He meets Constantijn Huygens again, poet, composer and secretary to the Prince of Orange. He examines snowflakes under the magnifying glass. He argues that light spreads instantly from our bodies to our eyes. He writes letters and more letters.

The effort of so much observation and writing hurts his eyes, and he must give them a rest after increasingly shorter periods. He gazes at the sky through the window, and the shift in focus brings relief to the muscles in his head and neck. Many times, he finds himself deep in thought, observing the tiny specks of dust that swirl in the air and collide with each other. He must pull himself back into action.

Meanwhile, the affection between the philosopher and the maid surges like a cloudy and implacable tide that laps at the walls of reason until it undermines them from their foundation.

One day, he says to her, 'I see you can read and write.'

'Yes, my father sent me to one of the schools in town. I have no brothers and my poor father has been cursed with three female daughters, but he has always been very good to us. I am the older sister, and when I was little, I helped my mother take care of my sisters. I also cared for my mother during her illness, and now that she is gone, I have become like a mother to my siblings. Because of this, my father decided to send me to study, even though it was a great effort for him, since I couldn't help him with the chores around the house. Then I practiced writing at the house of one of my mistresses. It was one of my first jobs. A very good lady, but with bad eyesight and arthritis in her hands. So, I wrote letters for her and read books to her. The other servants were jealous of me at first, but then I started writing letters for them as well. I was there for almost three years until the mistress became seriously ill, and I had to find another residence in which to work.'

'I have a sister who I love with all my heart. I have not seen her for a few years, but she is very happy, and this knowledge fills me with calm.'

'I miss my sisters too. We must travel everywhere, looking for work. Sometimes we lose contact with each other, but once a month we meet at father's house and give him money. My father is a carpenter, but he suffered a serious illness and lost one of his legs. Now he can't work like before.'

'I never knew my mother, but I think about her. She's present all the time, even when I think of something else. I regret not remembering her face. There is no material when I think of her, except the love with which her body nurtured mine. As a child I suffered from attacks of melancholy. It took me a lot to overcome them, and these states of sadness always made me think of my mother. In a way they brought me closer to her, since I know she suffered from them too. It's as though our souls in those moments were united in a single feeling.'

'That's what should happen when people fall in love, isn't it? What mystery! The same passion inhabiting two bodies. I'm very happy to remember my mother, even when her absence makes me sad. I know it doesn't make sense, but I wonder why we can remember some things more clearly than others.'

'You see, Helena, our brains are full of little holes that, when they open and close, draw patterns in the inside walls. When we remember or perceive something repeatedly, the pores acquire a tendency to form that figure more easily.'

'Our head is full of holes? Now I can see why my ideas slip away so easily.'

Renatus laughs at the ceiling.

'I'd like you to write something.'

Helena looks at him strangely, and he raises his hands in the air as if offended. He offers her a blank piece of paper and dips the pen in the inkwell.

'What do you want me to write?'

'As love grows within you, so does beauty because love is the beauty of the soul.'

She laughs her crystal laugh, the laugh of a child. When she blushes, two perfect circles burn on her cheeks. She places the piece of paper on the table and writes. When she hands him the page, those two perfect circles glow like hot iron on her white ceramic skin.

'What beautiful handwriting! Neat, even and full of grace. And the curls in the letter *h* and the letter *r*—perfect!'

'You say such flattering things, Reyner.'

'I'm only telling the truth! Although few have ears to listen.'

The first winter in Amsterdam is exceptionally harsh, and Renatus can no longer take his daily walk due to the cold and ice. Helena suggests that he go skating on the canals, which will give him the same amount of exercise. He wonders how it is possible to measure the amount of exercise a body does. It is not as simple as putting two bodies on a scale and comparing weight. The idea is ridiculous, he decides.

In mid-winter, Renatus wakes with a fever. He has slept most of the day. He tries to call Helena, but he can barely make a sound. Before long, she knocks on his door and enters without waiting for an answer.

'You are awake! The Monsieur is very worried and so am I. You were talking in your sleep for most of the night. I could hear you from my room downstairs.'

With his back to the light, he stares at her with eyes that seem pitch black. She knows that they are dark brown and tries to remember that hue. What sad and deep eyes! Helena looks away abruptly and tilts her head.

'I haven't been sick in many years,' protests the philosopher. 'I don't have time to stay in bed!'

Helena brings him wine infused with tobacco, honey and mint, one of her homemade recipes. Renatus complains weakly but ends up ingesting everything she gives him. Helena brings him cloths soaked in icy water to lower his fever, and he accepts her care like a child. She tells him that he must not tire himself, that the letters and his animal experiments can wait, and that the new light of spring will allow him to finish his treatise.

In the afternoons, when her duties allow her a few moments of rest, she goes to Renatus's room and fills the jars with water. She holds them against the light, catching that certain time in the afternoon when sunlight streams directly through the window.

Observing the patterns of coloured light on the wall, Renatus momentarily forgets his pains. She sits on the bed close to him. This has long become a habit. Renatus feels the hammering of his heart, the blood pounding in his ears. The closeness of her body seems to increase his fever; however, it also transforms it into a strangely pleasant state.

Every time Helena leaves, the philosopher's gaze drains of all life, and he loses himself within. The beauty of a woman can dazzle reason and make it falter. It has already happened with a certain woman. He was young and very stupid back then.

Helena, like Helen of Troy. Even the Greeks were prepared to die in war for a woman. We haven't learned anything.

He sits at the desk. He squeezes the wax between his fingers and looks at the imprint of his thumb. He thinks of the heart, its fire without light. The shadow of Helena's memory lingers in the room, and he can perceive the sweet and distant scent of her body. But he is not alone.

'You can't stop thinking about her, Renatus.'

He refuses to look up and thus lend realness to the stranger.

'A woman would be a drag on my life, and I must continue my work. I can't succumb to the passion I feel for this simple and modest woman.'

'But there is nothing wrong with love, as long as reason also approves of its object and that it is not a mere carnal appetite.'

'How can one tell the difference? In a way, Helena is ideal for me, so honest and pure, so oblivious to the artificiality and high expectations that characterise the women I have known and, on some occasions, awkwardly courted.'

'It's true, Renatus. These noble women confuse the appearance of virtue with virtue itself and follow the commands of society as if they had been decreed by God Himself. So, why don't you follow the advice of your passions?'

Then the stranger leaves as suddenly as he arrived.

A week later, Renatus wakes. He is feeling much better, and she is by his side. He is not sure what time it is, but it is day. He is certain that Helena should not be here but shaking the rugs or sweeping the floors. Yes, it is almost noon, he can tell, and she is in her nightgown. What is happening? She looks skinnier without her skirts.

The soft, fleshy, sweet shape against his forehead is Helena's cheek. The philosopher finds himself with his chin sunk between the woman's breasts. He can barely breathe, but he has neither the will nor the desire to resist.

'You're so good to me.'

It is Helena's little voice. He can feel her warm breath on the skin, but Renatus also feels something cold and wet against his face. It takes him a few moments to infer that Helena is crying.

He manages to push her away, sitting with difficulty against the headboard. *Why are you crying?* he wants to ask her, but the words flounder in his dry throat. His head is suddenly very clear, although his body is shaking uncontrollably. He tells himself, *I must be strong*, but the shaking does not seem to come from him.

He takes Helena's pale, chubby hand, feeling the rough skin from so much washing and working. He squeezes it between his hands, as if he wants to cut through the flesh and feel the substance, its essence, the soul itself. Sensing that he is going to fade again, he fights with the tides that drag him away. He tries to swim to the surface. He must keep himself dignified and composed.

Oh, those beautiful eyes.

Upon regaining consciousness, Renatus finds himself reclining on a pile of pillows. Where is Jean? That rascal. Then he remembers that he sent him on a trip.

He recalls what happened and sees Helena next to him holding his hands. She has fallen asleep in a chair next to his bed. There is ice in the centre of his bones, but his flesh is boiling. It is the fever again.

Helena opens her eyes. 'I beg your pardon. I didn't mean to bother you.'

'Be quiet, please. I'm fine.'

His voice is somewhere between a snore and a whisper. Helena leans forward and kisses his forehead, then his lips and cheeks. They are rough, hungry, wet kisses. Renatus feels himself fading again.

'What are you afraid of?' she says.

'I'm not afraid. It's that a few years ago I swore that I would never establish romantic ties with a woman.'

'What happened? Let me guess. A lady broke your heart.'

'It's not that. I think I broke hers. It's not something of which I am proud. How can I explain? Love is a complex matter, governed by arbitrary conventions, formalities and rules without any logical ground or connection. They are rules that change according to the society in which one lives. It takes a long time to learn these rules, and then you feel like a prisoner of them. I need my privacy and freedom. I could not settle in some fixed place. I could not provide my wife with the time and affection that women demand.'

'It will be our secret, Reyner. Maybe you should listen only to your heart. Or your head, whichever you prefer.'

'I promise I'll take care of you, whatever happens. I am not a wealthy man, but I will make sure that you have decent work and that you never suffer from hunger or misfortune.'

'I love you very much, Reyner. You are a good man.'

'Please, Helena, I need to rest.'

'Should I call the doctor? It's just that there's no one home. I can't leave you alone. I'll get you some cold cloths.'

'I don't want to see a doctor! I need to sleep. Please understand me.'

Helena's eyes fill with more tears.

'You don't understand me,' he says, 'I need... Give me a kiss. One more kiss... Your mouth on my forehead helps lower the fever. Then tonight... Why don't you come tonight? Like every night…'

'Before that, I'll bring you your medicine and cold cloths. And tonight we have herring. Monsieur Sergeant has praised the herring, although his jubilation was probably the product of wine.'

Helena retires and the philosopher rises from the bed. He listens to the noises in the house. Dogs barking. The sound of pots, spoons and knives. The shakiness and dizziness have miraculously stopped. His legs feel stable and strong.

As he closes his eyes, he meets Helena's gaze, her pure and kind eyes. He has been the cause of her crying. Why do women cry so easily? He cannot allow himself this. He cannot succumb to passion. However, he has already done so, and now he only needs to ennoble his passion with reason. He can feel the contact of her skin, her lips on his forehead.

He goes to the window. The crowd is still there. Always the same crowd, although its components change and shift. The sound of carriages, merchants announcing their offers, children playing on the sidewalk. The blood hits the inner walls of his body, producing a gentle heat in the chest. Passions are part of our nature. We simply must avoid their excesses.

'We have seen enough by now, my dear Francine. Let us give our lovers a moment of privacy. Now the bells of the clock are ringing. One curtain closes and another one opens, and we must hasten our pace. I need you fresh and clear for the next Act in which you will occupy the central role. Our adventure has just begun!'

11

Where, to the further delight and instruction of the reader, the automaton represents scenes from the life of the true Francine.

One can sense the deep expanse of the room, its space unfolding beyond the limit of the senses. The abyss of death itself contemplates us from the beginning of life. The unborn child is already able to think and form corporeal ideas, and his soul possesses within it the ideas of God, mind, body, infinity, geometric shapes and all the notions that represent true, immutable and eternal essences. But the soul is so attached to matter that it cannot yet do anything except receive various impressions from the body. It confusedly perceives the ideas of pain, heat, cold and the passage of fluids within the body—the internal tingling of maternal nutrition.

The strongest and most immediate sensation is that of the fluids swirling around and caressing the surface of the bare skin, a skin that is not even skin yet, but a gelatinous cocoon composed of highly complex machines that weave the worldly substrate of the future flesh, the instrument of the soul. The eddies surround and appease the incipient mind, the mind without language, the mind that is just a pulse amid the flows, a knot of passions barely distinguished from the swells, swings and circulations of the environment.

Love is the first and main passion that our soul becomes aware of in those initial moments when it is united to the body. Here our first associations are born, which will last for the rest of our lives. Certain movements of the spirits are inextricably linked to the thoughts that accompany them. The maternal juice that enters the heart causes a heat that the soul perceives as beneficial, and thus the soul voluntarily binds itself to this food. That is, the soul *loves* it. The spirits flow from the brain, asking the stomach, liver and intestines to deliver more of this nutritious juice, and for the rest of our lives, love will be accompanied by a bodily heat around the heart.

> ...I help maman sweep and ventilate the rooms, then she dresses me in the blue dress, the cutest I have. She gazes at me for a long time in the mirror and it is as though she doesn't recognise me. She sobs and holds me tight until I can barely breathe. She says I'm growing like a cabbage.
>
> We say goodbye to Mrs Greta. The lady hugs us and gives us a basket with bread, fruits and honey. She promises that she will pray for us so that God will look after us during the trip. I'm hungry, it must be lunchtime by now, but I don't say anything. Our belongings are on the sidewalk, ready for the men to load onto the wagon. I sit down to wait on the steps. The most fun part of going to live in a new house is packing all my belongings. I have spread my dresses, coats, chemises and shoes on the bed and counted them before putting them in the trunk. The most special thing is the pearl necklace that papa brought me from a faraway place. Maman sometimes shows me the necklace, promising me that one day I will be able to put it on and look like a princess, and papa will take me by the arm to walk through the streets of a beautiful and immense city that is far away. I'd be happy if papa would take me for a walk in the meadows near the river, like we did last summer, looking for bugs and playing hide and seek. The last time he left, I told him I was going to feel sad, and he told me that you can feel happiness just by thinking about it. He told me that the secret is to think of nice things to take the place of sad things.
>
> Maman promises me that I will like the people in the new house, and that there will be more room to play inside on rainy days, but I will miss this place and those who are here. I close my eyes and try to think of something else, of the little silver fish that I saw in the river today...

The light casts a parallelepiped of light on the chequered mosaic floor. Standing with his back to the window, Descartes reads one of the many letters that have arrived this week. Kneeling a few steps from him, in the centre of the diamond of light, the girl makes a hat from a discarded leaf.

'You know Francinette, that the scribbles on this page were made by a goose.'

She emits a limpid and sweet laugh, like the clink of glass.

'Geese can't draw! They have no hands!'

'Correct. They also cannot solve geometric problems, and much less this goose! That, besides being a goose, is silly. I see you have made something useful out of these useless sheets. Is it for me?'

'Voilà! A hat for the rain. Here you go, Pa!'

The girl walks towards her father, her shadow lengthening in the stain of light. Descartes leans down to receive the hat.

'Merci, Francinette. You crown me like a knight. I swear to God and my country to serve my Queen Francinette! Right on time because I have more paper for you. Here, my dear. Even you can solve this. What will you do now?'

'A little animal.'

'Very good, Francinette. Which animal?'

'A bubugateau.'

'Oh! What is a bubugateau? I have never heard of it.'

'He lives in that place far away. That place you told me about where the animal with the very long neck lives.'

'Oh, sure! The place is called Africa. Come, why don't we look at the globe? Let's see if you can find Africa.'

…maman, papa, and I play a game where we pretend that the two of them aren't my maman and papa. Papa says I'm his niece, and maman is the maid. I tell everyone that he is my uncle. It's like playing hide and seek or making shadows. But Mrs Agnès looks at me in a peculiar way and I think she knows that it is a game, and her kind eyes want to tell me that she is playing too…

In the dark room, the philosopher waves and clasps his hands in front of the lamp. Near him, another living shadow, as small as a bird, is breathing. It is possible to even hear its eyes flicker. An unsteady yellow light is projected on the wall, where shapes of various creatures follow one another. A bird with enormous wings, a hare that points its ears towards them, a galloping horse, a butterfly, a deer, a rabbit. Each appearance induces the fragile tremor of the girl's laugh. Inside that little head, the subtle spirits draw figures that are like shadows of shadows. The imagination completes the shapes and brings them to life.

Now, gentle eddies of air bring other sounds. A soft snore, the light shuffling of legs. Judging from the way he perches his ears, Monsieur Grat, the dog, seems to recognise the figures on the wall and sometimes barks at them. The philosopher's hands stop mid-movement and the creature on the wall pricks its ears to listen. The girl hugs the animal, and he growls with pleasure.

...papa has a big room full of things that he doesn't want me to touch. He locks himself there all day and, in the afternoons, when it's not raining or very cold, he takes me for a walk along the riverbank. He shows me leaves, insects, rocks. He tells me that very simple principles can produce many different things. On Saturdays, after mass, we go on a picnic, the three of us, to a place next to the stream, under the trees. Papa changes when we are alone. He laughs out loud and even seems to walk differently. He teaches me to fight with branches, and he says that when I'm older he will teach me to fight with a sword. I prefer to look in the stream for fish. There are some very small ones, and when I try to grab them, they escape. Sometimes, if it's been raining, we go hunting for rainbows with papa. They always hear us approach and recede away or vanish suddenly. I was told that there is a big pot full of gold at the end of the rainbow, but papa tells me this is a lie. Rainbows are drops of water.

Maman tells me that papa sometimes does ugly things in his room and the backyard, things that children should not see. Once he and Clément, his assistant, and Pieter, one of the servants, were waiting in the yard for the butcher and then there was a horrible howl, like when they kill pigs or chickens, except that this scream lasted a long time, and maman decided to take me for a walk to the market so as not to hear the screams anymore. I'm very curious about what papa does in his room with the door closed. Sometimes I approach the door to see if I can hear something.

Monsieur Grat also seems to be interested in what papa is doing and stands in the doorway, wagging his tail. Mama says Monsieur Grat tries to eat papa's experiences. I don't really know what this means, but the important thing is that Monsieur Grat doesn't come into the room to eat papa's things. I like to pretend that Monsieur Grat is my horse. Every time I climb on him, he looks at me and smiles, showing his teeth and gums.

When papa goes away, they lock his room. Maman cleans it daily, but she won't let me come in with her to clean. Papa must think a lot, she says. It is what he does. He thinks about very difficult things and then writes down his thoughts. One time papa got really mad when I spilled a bottle of ink on his desk. When he's angry, he walks quickly from one side of his room to the other. He gets angry when the postman is late and often angry with people who are not there. He told me once that people write him stupid letters and send him stupid books that he never reads. Maman and I laugh because papa is very funny when he's angry. We laugh without him seeing us because if he saw us he would get even angrier. Papa shows me a long tube to see the stars. He says I'm ready to use it because I've already learned how to close one eye. He tells me to look at the moon and see if there are any animals there, but I don't see any. They are probably hiding because they think we will eat them.

Papa teaches me the difference between planets and stars. Planets do not twinkle like stars, and on clear nights, if you look closely, you can see their colours. I ask him if people live in the stars and he laughs, but then he tells me that it is very possible that there are people living on other planets but not in the stars because they are very hot. I ask him if anyone has ever counted all the stars in the sky and he tells me that one day someone will. He says we will be able to deduce the number, without counting them one by one…

'What makes blue and yellow?'
   'Green!'
   'What makes red and blue?'
   'Violet!'
   'Two plus two?'
   'Four!'
   'Cherry cakes in summer?'
   'Apple pies in winter!'

…this spring I am the pinxterbloom, the flower of Pentecost. We look for flowers in the marshland to decorate me. They dress me in white and the ladies of the town lend me their necklaces and pins. Then we collect coins. Gustaaf holds the train of my dress and can't keep up as we run from house to house. Then we go to Mrs Anna's bakery to buy pancakes and caramel-covered apples. Papa said that today is the day when the Holy Spirit visited the apostles and made them speak strange languages…

De la Vega grips the girl by the arm.

'Damoiselle Francine, it's time to leave. The work must continue. We are about to witness the most important Acts.'

'You can keep your work. I want to stay here and eat cherry pies in the summers and apple pies in the winters forever. You've said it yourself. It doesn't matter if this place is Hell as long as I can experience this happiness with my father.'

…on winter mornings, maman must get up to light the fire, and I hear her gasp in the freezing cold of the house. The boys from the other houses aren't coming out to play. They say that Gustaaf is very ill and that death wanders the town…

'We'll be back here, Francine. In fact, you never left. You are and always will be here.'

'My father is right. You are a liar.'

'Oh Francine, your words are like stabs in my heart! Francine? Come back here or you will get lost in this place. Damoiselle!'

12

Where the philosopher and his shadow engage in another of their discussions, this time around the nature of truth and illusion.

A faint sound is heard in the cabin. Startled, Descartes comes to himself. His gaze darts across the room. He glances at the trunk but knows the sound did not come from there.

'It's you. Again,' he says to the darkness. 'What brings you here? Are you coming to look for it? Take it, please.'

'Why do you always look around to check that you're alone? Are you afraid of something, perhaps?'

'Every day that passes, I'm afraid of less things. I'm cautious, nothing more.'

'Is that why you're going to seek refuge behind the skirts of the Swedish Queen? To live in the middle of the bears and the ice? You won't find what you are looking for there, you know it very well. To the Queen, you are but a toy, an ornament for her court.'

'We'll see.'

'Those years you shared with Helena and Francine were the happiest of your life. You relived the paradise of your childhood, this time through the lens of another childhood, that of your secret daughter. Tell me the truth, Descartes. Could you have written your *Meditations* any other way? Such a pure and orderly book, a book that brings to mind the image of a man alone, sitting calmly in his room, away from the responsibilities and daily hustle and bustle of the crowd. A self-confident man who is not afraid of the whirlwinds of extreme doubt.

'Except you weren't alone, no! Helena and Francine were the necessary condition of your loneliness. It's true, you had many good friends, but the intimacy a man enjoys in the company of women is very different. Your *Meditations* are not a soliloquy but a dialogue. And, actually, I was with you too. I am one of your most famous creations, and it was not even your intention. Are you listening to me, Descartes?'

'What you say may be true, but your truths are always mixed with lies to the point that it is impossible to separate them. You said that device in the trunk would help me recover. You said it would be the most irrefutable demonstration of my ideas. You know, I don't know if I feel the pain anymore. I don't know if it's still there or if it has spread throughout the world to become an intimate part of all things. This pain that started in my heart took over my whole body and soul until it became difficult to lift my pen to write. Over time I convinced myself that the pain was gone, that I had finally managed to overcome it; however, all you have done is immortalise it.'

'Oh, Descartes, you are the one who lies to yourself. I see the pleasure you take when you play with Francine.'

'That thing isn't Francine!'

'Careful, Descartes! She is listening to us. You will hurt her feelings. She only appears to be sleeping, but even in their dreams the machines are constantly awake. I know very well what you will tell me: that the automaton only deceives the senses, that this device, as you call it, is like a cane that has helped you regain the ability to walk, but that you no longer need it. However, is your joy, the peace you feel in her presence, a mere appearance? A simulacrum? How could you perceive the difference if there was one?'

'I'm not in the mood for these games. Don't you ever sleep? Don't you have better things to do than torment me?'

'Let me illustrate my point with a fable. Would you allow me? It's the fable of a man awaiting the return of his beloved, who has been absent for a long time due to some family problem. Day after day, this man from my modest sobering tale sits in front of his house looking at the undulating road that disappears on the horizon. Now, suppose that, on any given morning, the yearning man finally perceives the image of his beloved approaching, except that this image is a mere product of the sunlight's refraction. Suppose it had rained heavily the night before and that blankets composed of tiny drops of water hang in the air, producing illusory images. Isn't the passion that the man feels, at that moment for the image of his beloved, a true and genuine feeling?'

'You speak nonsense. The man has arrived at a wrong judgment. The cause of his happiness is not true. Therefore his happiness is not true since it does not correspond to anything real.'

'What if his beloved had been replaced by an automaton that imitates her perfectly? Suppose that his beloved has perished during the journey, and that some wise and pious inventor decided to engineer a machine that cannot be distinguished from the living original. The man lives like this, happy for the rest of his days, thinking that he has reunited with his beloved and that the machine is truly his mistress.'

'You are a clumsy sophist. The answer is obvious—the man's judgment is still wrong. He has lived happily because of an illusion. It's the same case as with the optical illusion.'

'Is there any way the man can know that he has been deceived?'

'I see where all this is going. It is *absolutely true* that he has been deceived and that his happiness does not deserve such name, even when it cannot be distinguished from the happiness that he would feel in the company of his true beloved.'

'However, consider the following argument. Suppose that the man experienced the passion of love as undeniably authentic. It does not matter that in the future he realises his mistake, since his subsequent disappointment will not take away the certainty of her presence. I think, I exist. What is thought but an indication of existence? Does it not follow from this that existence is the most primary and fundamental fact and that it precedes thought?

'In which case pure existence is what counts, and nothing can deny my experience. Nothing can deprive lived experience of its authenticity. Nothing can deny it because love is, after all, *lived* and not *known* or *thought*. I have observed the abandon with which you surrender to your memories. Aren't these memories mere appearances—false by definition? You know the truth and at the same time you surrender to your illusory happiness, even if only occasionally and reluctantly. But that happiness is the same as you felt in the presence of the real Francine. Can we judge the authenticity of the passions according to their causes? Does it really matter if the causes are true or not?'

'If it were up to you, men would live in a great illusion, thinking that they wear silk clothes and gold-embroidered shirts, when in reality they are wearing filthy rags. Men would think that their monarchs are just and noble people, while they are really tyrants of the worst kind. I'm fed up already. *Again.* And here I am again, talking to myself!'

13

Which deals with the saddest and most tragic event in this work.

A better recipe than prolonging life through science is to stop being afraid of death.

—René Descartes

'Here you are, dear Francine! I've been looking everywhere for you. You must understand, my princess, your father needs you. You must perform your role in the play.'

'It's a very sad role. I already know what is coming now and I cannot bear it. I can't bear to play death over and over.'

'It is true that what follows is the most heart-breaking Act, but afterwards you can show yourself as you really are.'

'Then what? Didn't you just argue that who I am doesn't count? That the only thing that matters is the experience, not the reality?'

De la Vega, waiting patiently by her side, does not answer. On stage, the light fades to shadows. She hesitates for a long time as tears run down her cheeks. Finally, she closes her eyes and takes his broad, hard hand.

Mechanisms grind and snap into action. The racks on both sides of the stage display the image of a Greek temple. Skeletons cling to the columns in contorted, pleading and desperate poses. It is a temple of death. Two skeletons, one on each side, draw the curtains. One carries the whip of the plague and the other the hourglass of time. The portal above the stage represents a deep and dazzling sky, where angels flutter among the clouds, trumpets at the ready, observing with benevolent curiosity the actions taking place in the world below, in the theatre of mortality. Onstage, the illusory space of the temple is extended and transformed into the scenic space of a room.

In the centre of the room, there is a bed. On it, at the vanishing point where the stage lines converge, lies a pale and dying girl. Her reddened, half-open eyes stare elsewhere, a world far away from this one. The girl's features are difficult to distinguish, even though candlelight illuminates her. Shadows clump around her, their postures parodying those of the skeletons. The shadow of a woman kneels beside the girl in prayer position, her face buried in the sheets. Even the girl seems to be another shadow, made of dark light. She lifts a silver chalice to heaven, her eyes raised slightly to contemplate eternity.

Descartes is in the city of Leiden supervising the printing of the *Meditations* when the messenger arrives at the house where he is lodged. They set off immediately. The trip takes just over two hours at a brisk gallop.

He arrives to find Helena waiting for him at the door. Their gazes meet for an instant, then flinch as if avoiding direct sunlight.

Upon entering the room, Descartes prostrates himself by the bed without paying attention to those present. He places a palm on the girl's chest. She seems so small, sunken in the bed. Her eyes are closed, and he can barely feel her breath. The heartbeat is both weak and fast. He feels suddenly exhausted, as though he has been bled excessively. His throat closes and tears congeal. Sadness cools the blood and constricts the body's pores, while love causes the heart to push more blood through the arteries.

Around him, a dance of shadows and half-faces. The world has lost substance. He could be in a dream, but he certainly is not. He distinguishes two girls and a boy, the same age as Francine. Their faces carry a mixture of fear and anguish. In a corner of the room, Descartes spots the schoolmaster, a young man sitting in a chair, clutching a Bible and muttering a droning prayer. There is an older woman, hunched over and dressed in dark colours, with a black scarf covering her hair. They are all unknown to him. Even Helena seems to be a stranger.

And Francine! Recognising his beloved girl requires a painful effort of the imagination. Descartes holds her rough, swollen hand covered in red pustules. The exposed parts of the skin are lined with the same rash, except for a triangular area around the mouth. The cheeks burn with a dark red fire, and the lips are dry and withered. Descartes feels guilty about leaving her like this. He feels guilty for having abandoned her, for not having recognised in time the seriousness of Francine's condition.

Three days ago, when he received the news of the first fever, Descartes sent Helena a series of instructions. Lower the fever with wet cloths, then administer a mixture of cider and rue decoctions, plus a little milk with honey. He begged Helena not to allow bloodlettings, but he's sure the imbecile doctor did it anyway. He, René Descartes, despite all his knowledge, cannot cure a simple fever.

He rests his hand on Francine's chest, detecting a slight tremor.

'My dear Francine,' he whispers. 'Can you hear me?' He turns to the others. 'We need air. Open a window!'

Someone says that it is cold; however, the schoolteacher promptly opens a window. It is growing dark. The lady in black is busy lighting candles and placing them on tables and shelves. A gust stirs the flames, and the light in the room flickers, swaying on the edge of darkness.

Descartes squeezes Francine's hand. Beneath its guise of flesh and skin, the girl's life ebbs slowly and loses momentum. He cannot even say goodbye to her properly, or look into her eyes one last time, or feel the presence of her restless, lively soul.

Helena asks everyone to leave them alone for a few moments.

Descartes looks to the doorway and his heart skips a beat. Francine is standing there. No, it is another girl, very similar, though older, about ten or twelve. Is it Francine's soul? So soon? In the blink of an eye, the image fades as merciful tears cloud his vision.

'Don't go,' he whispers. 'If you are listening to me, dear, please don't leave us.'

From an abysmal distance, he watches his tears fall onto the sheets and onto his shirt, an apparently inexhaustible quantity. He hears a broken cry and realises that it is coming from him. Passions overflow his body, and he seeks petty consolation in the idea that those who cry easily have a deeper capacity for love and pity.

My Francine, my little one, my adored Francinette.

The fever drops and he can no longer feel the tremors. He squeezes her hand forcefully, as though he can contain the breath of life flushing from her. The muffled breathing recedes into nothing. The hand is matter now, nothing else, becoming still.

Are you already gone, my Francine?

Descartes chokes on his own tears. The passions quiver through him as though they are tearing his body apart from within. He perceives, diffusely, the streams of dried tears on the girl's cheeks, her face turning to stone.

Helena leans over Francine and hugs her. Her crying is more like a howl. The mother's face sinks into the girl's chest. Descartes attempts to conjure a last prayer for the girl's soul.

'In the name of the angels, archangels and prophets, of the holy apostles and evangelists, of the holy martyrs, confessors, monks and hermits, of the holy virgins and all the saints of God, peace be with you today, and may your home be in Heaven. Through Christ our Lord. Amen.'

The words sound hollow, but it would be arrogant to think that we can know the inscrutable designs of God.

I cannot help but conceive that those who die go to a more pleasant and serene life than ours, and that one day we will go to meet them.

The prayers are lost in the deep and silent abyss, where the peace of the soul and the nothingness of death merge and are confused. The tears are gone, and the crying is a dry gasp. Shyly, the mourners return to the room. Others join them. The local priest prepares his instruments on a table next to the bed.

Francine is peaceful now. She could be sleeping. If the amount of motion in the universe is constant, then the motions that animated this child's body will become part of the world. The flickering of her thoughts will feed the flow of the rivers, the beating of her little heart will add impetus to the wind, and the motion of her hands learning to embroider will make the leaves of the trees grow.

Now, it is dark, and someone has closed the window. The priest murmurs a prayer. Someone says that they must move the body before the soul passes to the mattress. Helena's hand closes over his and he feels something on his palm. It is the pearl necklace. Descartes looks at it for a moment, then places it around his daughter's cold neck.

The stage darkens and de la Vega leads Francine around the back of the timber decking.

'The angels are crying,' he says, and his words only make the sadness deeper. He searches his pockets for another handkerchief, crimson this time. He leads Francine from the stage and into the gloom. They pass a familiar tableau: a man in a nightgown playing with the golden-haired girl. They hear the rhythmic clapping, the weaker claps repeating the pattern of the stronger ones.

Clap clap tap *tap* clap *clap clap*.

The girl in the tableau emits a tiny laugh. She turns to the audience. Her face is half finished, exposing a dense knot of tubes. The audience sees the copper structure of her insides and her crystal eyeballs. They see the small bellows within her that inflate and deflate.

The crying resumes with great eagerness. De la Vega leads Francine to a chair, helping her to sit. He waits for her to calm down. She realises they are in another tableau.

The new setting is familiar. It is Uncle Ferrand's library in Châtellerault. Francine stares blankly at the rows of books. Her spirits settle down gradually. Her hand wrings the handkerchief, the only reminder of the sadness just experienced. The chimes are heard again. She closes her eyes and refuses to count them.

De la Vega moves towards the shelves as gently as his hobble allows. With a sharp glance, he extracts a slim tome from a row of books.

'Do you remember what I told you? I was able to save many of the writings in your father's trunk, the same trunk that Descartes entrusted to those rascals.'

Francine is not listening. With great care, de la Vega places the book on her lap. She raises her gaze to look at the man suspiciously, as if seeing him for the first time. She accidentally reads the title: *Breviter Collecta Litterarum*.

She opens it and is carried away.

14

Consisting of the Breviter Collecta Litterarum—*the correspondence between Helena, Francine's mother, and Rêver, also known as the genium malignum, and by many other names, including Señor Don de la Vega.*

Noble Monsieur,

It was a delightful surprise to receive Your letter, and I beg you to grant me Your forgiveness for the delay in composing a reply. You honour me by writing to me, and I am honoured to be able to assist You in Your request. I confess that this is the fourth or fifth time I have tried to answer You. I hardly ever receive letters, and Your words are so fine and beautiful, worthy of the ears of a queen, that I am ashamed to repay them with these strokes that You will surely judge blunt and lacking in elegance.

You can excuse the language of a simple woman used to writing inventories and lists of expenses and orders, although often the townspeople come to me to help them write letters to their loved ones or debtors or to read a letter aloud. Jans says I should charge for the service, but the enormous joy that this task brings is reward enough. I find in writing a respite from the daily routine and the complaints of my body.

Please pardon me for telling You these unimportant details, but it is that in my soul I feel close to You even though we have never met in person. I beg You then to excuse my ignorance of the proper ways in which to address Your Gentleness but be assured that I am Your humble servant and that I am at Your complete disposition.

At Your request, I have delivered to the valet of Monsieur D. the two packages that You have sent with Your letter. The Monsieur has received them, and I hope you will get a swift reply. You tell me that You have tried to contact Monsieur D. on two occasions and that You have not received a response. I advise You, with all due respect, that my knowledge of these matters is imperfect and my influence very limited. I understand that You are impatient, but do not doubt that I will impart word to You as soon as Monsieur D. deigns to receive me. You can also address Your missives to the tavern, with the assurance that they will be delivered to the Monsieur.

The Monsieur has returned very tired from his trip to France last summer. I have not seen him in a long time, since the day of my wedding ceremony, almost a year ago. Sometimes we send him gifts—a pot of honey, a rabbit, a basket of bread—and almost every week his valet comes to buy supplies. But you know that this is a small town where gossip circulates fast, and we know through long tongues that the Monsieur is somewhat downhearted. It seems that certain very important philosophers in our universities have mounted a smear campaign against our dear Monsieur, and this has him in a very bad mood. No one knows the details of these disputes, since no one here could understand the lofty questions that concern our great doctors. However, let me suggest to You that perhaps this is the reason why Monsieur D. has not yet been able to give Your previous letters the attention they undoubtedly deserve.

With Your permission, I must now rest and no longer delay the sending of this letter. I will keep you posted on any news.

Your humble servant,
Helena Jansz Van Wel

Noble Monsieur,

I beg Your apology for writing to You so promptly without having yet received Your reply to my last letter. The reason for this missive is to notify You of my visit to the residence of Monsieur D. this coming Saturday. Apparently, Monsieur D. wishes to see me, and to tell the truth I have missed the Monsieur. It is Jans's birthday next week, so I'll take the opportunity to personally invite Monsieur D. to the celebration. As you may know, the Monsieur does not want his birthday to be known, so Jans and I have decided that we will give him the appropriate gifts and celebration on Jans's own birthday.

I will ask the Monsieur about Your gift and relay the news to You. But please I beg You to understand that it would be impossible for me to intercede on Your behalf. My soul is a simple soul, accustomed to living among mere appearances, ignorant of the deeper truths behind the world. I hope you receive a quick response from the Monsieur by his own hand.

Your humble servant,
Helena Jansz Van Wel

Noble Monsieur,

I must confess that it is difficult for me to treat you informally, as you ask. My eyes filled with tears when I read your last letter, and I had to interrupt the reading many times. You should not waste such wise words, not to mention expensive ink and paper, on a simple mind like mine. In any case, I will treasure your words forever, and your advice will give me light in my hours of sadness. You have a deep understanding of a woman's soul. You say that all men and women are born with the same nature, some stronger, others wiser, but all forged in the same image of an Almighty and perfect God, full of love for His creation.

If you allow me to digress, your words have reminded me of something Monsieur D. told me some time ago when I was in his service. He told me that all men are born with the light of reason, and that the light is the same in all souls, even in that of women. This light must be cultivated and cared for, since all evil and sin are born out of ignorance and laziness. On several occasions, displaying his noble spirit, Monsieur D. has taken into his residence simple peasants who were eager to learn the principles of his mathematical method, and with great generosity he instructed them in these matters.

It is true what you say: it is our duty to have children and populate the earth as God has commanded us and teach them well and instruct them to distinguish good from evil. These words have touched me closely since I am expecting my first child. May God grant me a boy, is all I ask! I am starting to show my belly and I am tired of standing. Your sweet words and advice have relieved my fatigue and lit the light of my faith, for which I owe you my eternal gratitude. I must confess that sometimes I am so afraid. I have not done anything good or special in my life and I want this child of mine to please God. I want him to grow up healthy and strong, and to be able to handle himself in this uncertain and disappointing world.

How happy I am writing to you! My anguish disappears and my pains drain away from my soul. You do not have to apologise. Your command of the Dutch language is extraordinary and shows once again the exquisite sensitivity and intelligence of your person. In fact, you write in my mother tongue better than me.

I must now address the reason for this letter. I hope you can excuse my deviations and distractions. On Saturday I spent a pleasant day at the residence of Monsieur D., who has been very interested in the content of your previous shipment, and who says he remembers you from his student days. I will not bore you with the details of the visit, but you should know that I have mentioned, in a very discreet way, the fact that you have written to me. I pointed out to the Monsieur that your letter concerned other matters, related to the laws of the municipality and inquiries about accommodation. At the mere mention of your name, the Monsieur was very excited. I told him I could find you accommodation. Of course, not in the tavern, which is a very rustic place and unworthy of His Gentleness. Monsieur D. has given me a letter for you, which I am enclosing. I suggest you wait for the end of winter before traveling.

At your disposition, etc.

Helena

Noble Monsieur,

I do not know how to thank you in words for the gift you have sent me. The pens, the handkerchiefs and the little ink bottles are very beautiful. I am using one of the pens you have given me, which seems to glide effortlessly across the paper. It is as if the pen writes on its own! The paper is like silk, and I am ashamed to spoil it. Sorry, I started crying, but you are so generous.

I can smell a sweet and distant fragrance on the handkerchief that brings back vague memories and incites in me a disposition that is both melancholic and happy. Monsieur D. has asked me about you, and I have arranged the details of your visit. The Monsieur agrees that the date is auspicious. We are preparing a room for you, a comfortable and clean place out of direct sunlight as you have requested. I hope that our humble tavern is to your liking, and trust that I will do my best so that you find the stay to your liking.

You tell me that you are writing a manual on Cartesian philosophy, which will be preceded by a biography of the

Monsieur. You flatter me again with your opinion of me, but I am afraid I will not be of much help. You know that I have served Monsieur D. for many years. I can vouch that the Monsieur is a generous, noble and honest man. He has always treated us servants with respect and affection. Monsieur D. also generously helped with our wedding. These are just some of the facts that testify to the greatness of his spirit. I cannot tell you more than this. It is all that modesty, discretion and good manners allow me, and Monsieur D. is very jealous of his privacy. I wish you celebrity and immortality for your work.

It is so pleasant to write with the materials you have sent me! I do not feel fatigue when writing. You are so kind. We wait for you with open arms.

At your disposition, etc.

Helena

Noble Monsieur,

I cannot express to you how agreeable your visit has been. The mark of an excellent gentleman is the way he treats those who are below his class. If you allow me to give you some advice, you should not be ashamed of your physical ailments. All our fortunes and misfortunes are God's work, and we must accept them as part of His intentions. God has given you the blessing of a loquacious and exquisite tongue, and the way you express yourself has left us in awe. You can make the simplest of minds believe that they are penetrating the innermost secrets of philosophy.

You have been so kind to give me advice on how to write well. You have moulded my soul into something finer and more beautiful, and I will follow your directions like those of a wise teacher. I will use short sentences, without elaborate words, leaving aside my feelings and passions. You know, it is hard to do that, harder than to treat you informally.

At your request, I promise to keep you informed of any news concerning Monsieur D. It is rumoured that the Monsieur is looking for new lodgings, not far from here. I do not know the details of the 'experience' you mean. To tell the truth, I do not even know what that word means. On the other hand, I assure you that little Gert is fine, and that her parents, whom I have seen in the markets the day before yesterday, are very happy with the generous remuneration you have given them. The girl was a bit sad at first and was afraid that the other children would tease her because of her lack of hair. But they have given her some beautiful caps to hide her baldness, and her hair has already started to grow back.

As for our boy, he is growing up healthy and strong. God has blessed us, and I thank Him every day in my prayers. We are going to miss you, and I will miss writing to you. I will keep your presents as the most precious things in the world. I remain at your disposition for whatever you need.

Attached to this letter are some gifts. I hope they are to your liking.

Your humble friend and servant,
Helena

Noble Monsieur,

You will not receive this letter, but I am writing to you anyway because I have no one to turn to. The mere act of writing brings rest and hope to my soul. The words bring order to my thoughts, and it does not matter anymore if I am writing to myself. Perhaps this devilish pen and ink are the authors rather than the instruments of my thoughts.

Is this a confession? Yes, I have sinned, we have all sinned, but may God have the mercy to take us in His arms, His dear creatures. Those are things of the past, products of the carelessness of an innocent girl, things that I have tried very hard to forget. Anyway, my husband Jans has always known what happened, as well as my family and close friends. I tell myself that there is nothing to be ashamed of and that I must also think about Reyner's reputation. I am told that in order to slander him, one of the theologians has mentioned the rumours about an illegitimate daughter. So, I must be careful. On the other hand, I could not talk about the past without my passions intruding and making my task impossible.

I pray to God and ask Him to give strength to my soul. God and I will be the only ones who will know. I will also remember your advice to write short, direct sentences and put my passions aside. I will condemn this letter to the fire as soon as it is finished. It will be our secret.

I must confess that the first time I saw Reyner when he returned from his trip, his appearance caused me concern. Like I have told you, I had not seen him in a while. It was mid-afternoon and he had just arisen. He seemed smaller than I remembered, but perhaps I am the one who is bigger. He was wearing the same black silk nightgown that he has worn for years, with his cape and wig on to ward off the cold in the hallways. I noticed that his wig was streaked with white, and something in my expression must have betrayed my curiosity because, upon seeing me, Reyner took his wig off for a moment and I could see that now his hair is also grey as well as sparse. He told me that he had asked his wigmaker to add white hairs. This amused me and I tried to hide a smile. Reyner smiled at me too and this calmed me down a bit.

We spent a few pleasant hours in each other's company, mostly talking about small things. Reyner is studying the medicinal properties of certain plants. He showed me his garden and a beautiful catalogue of plants that he had brought from Paris. He told me that he was very happy to be back, and it seemed to me that his trip had disappointed him.

Of course, during your visit, I respected your request to leave you two alone while you carried out your 'experience.' Meanwhile, rumours reached me of what was happening at the residence. I heard that the servants, Ludolf and Anneke, had moved into the house at the back, which was used for storage until then. Meals were to be served in the kitchen at precisely specific times, and the valet was prohibited from entering the main room. Anneke told me that strange sounds were sometimes heard coming from there, and that it seemed to her that you and Reyner were practicing songs in a strange language. None of this seemed out of the ordinary to me. Reyner is always absorbed in his work, and he is obstinate in protecting his privacy. When I was in his service, it was common for Reyner to receive visitors and lock himself in with them for long hours, ignoring mealtimes and conversing late into the night. It occurred to me that Reyner was afraid someone might try to steal one of his inventions.

When you left, I tried to find some excuse to visit Reyner. I was worried about him, although perhaps what drove me was mere curiosity. I learned that Ludolf's niece, Catherine, spent some afternoons at Reyner's residence, helping in the kitchen and laundry. She is a very beautiful ten-year-old girl with luminous and restless eyes. I've always had a lot of affection for her. With her father's permission, I offered to teach her to embroider, and in this way, I began to frequent Reyner's residence twice a week. I always carried gifts, of course: preserves, cheese, fresh bread, a liquor, a tablecloth or whatever useful thing I could find. In the mid-afternoon, Catalina and I sat under the dining room window to embroider, taking advantage of the best hours of daylight. Most of the time I did not see Reyner, or we passed each other by with little more than a greeting, but sometimes he would sit with us for a while and talk. At first, I did not notice anything out of the ordinary. Reyner was still running his vegetable and herb gardens, and Pietr was watching over the hatching of eggs. In the afternoons, they would lock themselves in the dining room to open the eggs and examine them under a lens. After a few weeks I had to interrupt my visits due to the birth of my son, but I resumed the embroidery sessions as soon as I felt sufficiently recovered. It was then that I started to notice strange things. First, I thought I heard a sound in Reyner's room. I swear it was the voice of a girl. It seemed to me that she was imploring, that it was an ex-clamation full of anguish. I froze. It was as though I had sensed that sound with my body instead of hearing it with my ears. I felt a shooting pain in the pit of my stomach. I was very still, trying to pick up some other sound. I do not know how long I was there. Then Reyner appeared down the hall. He seemed to be in a good mood.

'Are you leaving now Helena?' he said. 'Are you feeling alright? Why don't you lie down and have a rest?'

I told him that Jeroen had the carriage ready and that I could not wait any longer, which was true. On the way to the tavern, and for the remainder of the day, I could only think about what I had heard. I was feeling very upset and tried to calm myself down. It was nothing, I told myself, just my imagination. Perhaps it was the wail of an animal that Reyner had trapped in there to make his observations.

The next visit was uneventful. Catalina told me that she was in love with Hans, the butcher's apprentice. And in the kitchen, Ludolf told me that Reyner was working on something very secret. He also told me that they were waiting for the visit of a Countess or Baroness. He was not sure. The lady would stay with them for a while to receive lessons in mathematics and philosophy from Monsieur D. Anneke was very nervous about the visit. They had to pay close attention to the house, and keep it clean and comfortable, and they were not sure what they were going to cook.

'Surely,' Ludolf said, 'a person of such distinction will have a very fine palate and will expect meals of the highest quality. And the Monsieur has us used to preparing boiled vegetables, bread and fish!'

I asked him if the Monsieur had already received a visitor, but he said no one had come since that 'strange man'.

'Please don't tell the Monsieur this,' he said 'but Anneke was terrified of the Monsieur's friend. I thought the lord was the devil himself! Me, on the other hand—I liked him. The man told me that he had come from very humble beginnings and that his hands had been deformed in that way because he had worked as a child in his father's smithy.'

The second disturbing episode took place at the end of my next visit. I was on my way to the carriage when I had the impression that I was being watched. Turning my head, I thought I saw that the curtains in Reyner's room had moved, as if someone was hiding behind them. An icy sensation ran through my body, but this time I hastened my steps. I felt that I should get away from there as soon as possible. Over the next few days, I thought again about what I had seen and tried to reason with myself. Was it possible that Reyner was hiding a lover? The idea was ridiculous, of course, but I clung to it to quell my unease.

Since then, I have visited Reyner's residence three times, after which I have resolved not to return nor to have anything to do with the Monsieur again. I hope you understand my motives. Even if I cannot disclose certain aspects of the past, something tells me that you know very well what I mean. Similarly, although you will never receive this letter, I suspect that you are already reading it.

On the next two visits, while Catalina and I did our embroidery, I listened carefully to the sounds of the house. Reyner was in his room and the servants were mostly silent. A little while later, I heard a murmuring and interrupted my duties. I recognised the voice instantly. It was sweet and transparent, repeating the same sound over and over, like a girl learning a new word. The voice brought back sad memories of things I had not thought about in a long time.

I decided to investigate. I knocked on the bedroom door and, while waiting, tried to make up some excuse. Perhaps I could offer him something to eat. After a while, Reyner opened the door and looked at me questioningly. He was tired and worried. All I could think to say was, 'Are you okay?' To which he nodded slightly, although I do not think he heard me. I tried not to look inside the room. I did not want to be nosy. I do not remember what we said to each other. Finally, Reyner dismissed me with a slight, forced smile.

Yesterday was my last visit. This time the girl did not try to hide but walked openly around the house. She was introduced to me as the Baroness of something. I was so moved that I did not catch her name, but I am sure that whatever it was is not her actual name, just as I am sure that this is all your doing.

Why? I am afraid to ask you. I feel cheated and I beg God to grant me the power to forgive you. Maybe once the anger subsides, I could do it. I know Reyner is not guilty and that he is a victim, just like me.

Short sentences, you said, impressions without passions.

She was in appearance an ordinary girl of about twelve years of age, but there was something in her. My beloved girl. Not physically, but something else. Have you trapped Francine's soul in that body? Her soul deserves to rest! Her soul deserves Heaven. Why have you called her from there?

The girl looked at me as though she recognised me. The look in her eyes told me that we shared a secret. But what horrified me the most was recognising that hair—the golden hair of Gert. I am certain of this!

I am also sure that Reyner realised what I was thinking because he accompanied me to the carriage.

'My dear Helena,' he said, 'I only want happiness for you. I have taken care of you, as I have promised. God forgive me for not being able to have...'

He could not finish the sentence. I was moved. For a moment I thought that he would start crying. I wanted to touch his cheeks, to comfort him, but it was not appropriate.

I do not think I am ever going to forget about that apparition. I hope to find strength in my heart to forget, to forgive, to move on. If what Anneke says is true, and you are the devil himself, I beg you to absolve me of your service, and I beg God to give me asylum in His abode. I will make a place in my prayers for Reyner.

I hope God will have mercy on us.

15

On how science helps human beings with the misfortunes of life.

We would be ascribing to the created creature the perfection of the creator if the creature could continue its existence independently of anything else.

—René Descartes

On the night of Rêver's departure, he dreamed of the flames again. In the theatre of his mind burns the eternal bonfire where Vanini and Bruno perish, where the books of Suárez and Galileo are consumed. Yellow wax-like faces clump in front of him. They speak to him all at once.

Rêver proposed that they exhibit the automaton in Paris. He suggested that they could take it to other cities as well, to Prague and Rome, for example. The experientia will be the most forceful demonstration of the ideas of the great philosopher Descartes: the body is a machine, and a soul is not required to operate its actions, even the most complex ones such as growth and digestion.

'Don't you think so, Descartes? It will also be a demonstration that, truly, it is nature that imitates art and not the other way around.'

'Will you turn my philosophy into a novelty show? If the automaton works as you promise, I will be considered a sorcerer, an alchemist. People will see the machine as a monstrosity, a trick of the dark arts, and the last thing I need right now is to enlist in more battles.'

'Perhaps you are right. Anyway, you have time to decide. I must go on a long journey. For now, take care of her, and make your observations and experiences. Talk to her, let her hear the voice of your thoughts and let her learn from you. You will see that little by little she will gain control of herself, and her abilities will surprise you. Don't be afraid to show her once she's ready. If you wish, we can announce that my niece, the Baroness of Chanteleux, will come for a season to study mathematics and astronomy with the revered philosopher. What do you think, Descartes?'

Helena comes to visit the day after. One of Jans's helpers brings her on his delivery route. She moves laboriously as she is pregnant again with Jans's child. Descartes kisses her on the cheeks and walks her by the arm into the main room. With surprising speed, Anneke serves beer, fruit, bread and cheese. The women talk to each other for a while, smiling and holding hands. Then Anneke excuses herself and leaves. Helena sits up with difficulty. They offer her the most comfortable chair, and Descartes brings cushions.

He tries to remember the last time he saw Helena. It was sometime before the arrival of Rêver. He does not remember what they talked about. Trifles, surely. Her presence is welcoming and flares up a distant affection. The passage of time has quenched the sorrow and pain. He regrets having considered Helena a mistake. Of all the women in his life, she shared his deepest intimacy as well as the greatest of pains. Francine is like another between them, a secret that unites them and at the same time drives them apart. It has been the most devastating sadness of his life, even more hurtful than the one caused by the deaths of his father and Jeanne.

'Did you get my note? I hope I'm not bothering you.'

'I have received it, thank you, and I've been waiting for you with great joy. You are always welcome here, you know that. You look very good, radiant. Happy as a young girl. Although I notice you seem somewhat tired. I hope Jans isn't making you work too hard.'

'Don't be concerned. Jans is very kind to me. I am working in the kitchen, the brewery and the garden, but only in the mornings. Then I work on the accounts and finances in the afternoons.'

'How much longer do you have now?'

Helena turns to face him and smiles. Her teeth are like opaque quartz. 'A month at the most.'

'It will be a summer baby.'

'Yes! We must take special care of him.'

Her gaze wanders for a moment. He waits in silence for her smile to return.

'Are they taking good care of you here? Are Anneke and Ludolf doing a good job?'

'I'm comfortable in this place and with the service, although I have forgotten to tell Anneke to light the fireplace. Are you cold?'

'I'm fine. I always throw on extra clothing, just in case. I must take care of my son. You know, René, every time I think of the child, I imagine a boy. I'm sure you have an explanation for this.'

Descartes emits a short, staccato laugh.

'My advice is that you should stay in good health and always think of things that are beautiful and rewarding. Your thoughts have an effect on the child. He can already form ideas. They are purely corporeal ideas, of course, produced without the intervention of the soul. But even so, the child can feel your kindness, your fear and above all your love. The love we feel in the womb is our first experience of passion.'

'I wonder where his soul is now.'

'There is no point in asking those things.'

'I was told that a woman recently gave birth to a dog. It seems that, on the night of conception, the husband was very drunk and threatened that he was going to sire a dog on her. And these words affected the woman in such a way that she did indeed give birth to a puppy.'

A warm blush flares on her cheeks and her lips widen into a nervous smile. Little holes appear in her cheeks, but Descartes detects a hint of fear in her eyes.

'That's nonsense! It is impossible. It goes against the order of nature. Don't fill your head with such garbage, dear. You have nothing to fear.'

He realises that he has raised his voice and gestured perhaps too vehemently. He takes a deep breath and tries to calm down. Helena has brought him a basket of cherries, a jar of honey and two fresh loaves of bread. Descartes gives her a medium-sized painting, a still life of food and wine glasses.

'It's going to look good in the tavern's dining room, don't you think? Don't worry, I obtained it at a very good price. The painter has a drinking problem and owes me some money.'

Descartes shows her the garden, and they talk about onions and carrots for a while. Soon after, Jans's assistant returns. Before saying goodbye, she mentions that she has received a letter from Rêver, who said he has not received a reply to the missives he sent to Descartes.

'If you write to Monsieur Rêver, tell him that I will reply shortly.'

But Descartes has not received any letters, and Rêver has made no effort to contact him. What is he playing at? Does he want to spread rumours among the townspeople and destroy the peace that the philosopher has worked so hard to achieve?

As the afternoon progresses, his feeling of annoyance turns to anger. He paces his room, glancing at the closed stove. When Ludolf comes to leave him dinner, he pretends to be working. He has many things to say to that rascal, Rêver; however, he would rather never see or speak to him again. He suspects that Rêver is trying to mislead him, that the reasons he has given in favour of the experientia are not his genuine motivations. He fears that it is himself, the philosopher, who is part of a more comprehensive experiment hatched by the mechanic.

He contemplates moving again, away from Helena and Rêver. But what to do with the automaton?

The machine has learned a new trick. Suddenly her gaze is fixed on him, looking right into his eyes. It is a mechanical reflex. If he moves his head to one side, the automaton's attention remains in the same position.

The girl appears to be sleeping with her eyes open. Her face is that of a finely sculpted statue. Her features are different from what he remembers of his beloved Francine. The brow and jaw are wider, rounder, and her lips are very thin. Her eyes are dark. She looks like a girl of about twelve or thirteen. That is a rhetorical effect, according to Rêver. The girl is an empty canvas where the philosopher's memories and desires are projected, like the passing images that we spot in the clouds.

Deep, contradictory passions tear him apart, leading him away from himself: longing, sadness, fondness, anger. In the morning, he reads the correspondence in bed, repeating passages out loud so that the machine can learn. His fingers hesitate for an instant before breaking each seal. The letters have fastidious surprises in store: objections, threats, criticism, slander, nonsense. He tries to answer each in detail, but his replies can't hide the tiredness and impatience he feels.

It is the end of spring, and in the afternoons his room is bathed for hours in crisp light. At the beginning of the afternoon, when Ludolf and Anneke return to the kitchen, he opens the door of the stove and sits down to write at his desk. The light falls obliquely on the stove's interior and illuminates the girl's face. After a while, the light wakes her, and her gaze falls on the pen.

'Are you awake? Your eyes move but can you see me? If only you knew the mess I'm in. They accuse me of being an atheist. I who have offered the most reliable and irrefutable proofs of the existence of God!'

Before long, his work absorbs him, and he forgets her. The pen glides firmly over the paper, betraying no trace of the tremors in his soul. He must not show any sign of weakness to these donkeys who are going out of their way to smear him and his system of philosophy. His words must be as clear and reasonable as the light of this room.

'The philosophy,' he writes, 'that I and my devotees are dedicated to follow is none other than the knowledge of those truths that can be perceived by natural light, and that can provide practical benefits for humanity. There is no study that could be more honourable in this life. The vulgar philosophy taught in schools and universities is, on the contrary, nothing more than a collection of opinions, for the most part dubious. No one has ever succeeded in obtaining any practical benefit from such false-hoods as "materia prima," "substantial forms," "hidden qualities" and the like.'

The quill stops. He can write for hours almost without realising, and these bursts of activity leave him increasingly drained. The pains accumulate in his back, shoulders and right hip.

He continues to take his walks, always after lunch. He searches for deserted paths and forests where it is easy to believe that he is completely alone in the world. At night he practices fencing, fighting his own shadow. The exercise helps dissipate the knots in his body, but the pains of the soul are another matter.

For these pains, he has received a balm, a blessing, a singular comfort: the correspondence with Princess Elizabeth of Bohemia. The words of the philosopher have never sounded clearer and stronger than in his responses to the concerns of this beautiful mind.

> Dearest Princess,
>
> Your very affectionate letter, showing that you have been thinking of me, is the most precious thing that could have happened to me in this country. Your letter is infinitely valuable, and I will take care of it the way misers take care of their treasures. The more they value them, the more they hide them from the rest of the world, and their supreme happiness is to behold them.

So, to answer your first question. The union of the soul and the body cannot be conceived only with the intellect, nor with the intellect with the help of the imagination. Yet the question becomes very clear when the senses come to our aid. People who never approach things in a theoretical way, and use only their senses, have no doubt that the soul moves the body and that the body acts on the soul.

They consider the soul and the body one thing. Recently, with an old friend from my childhood, an excellent craftsman and engineer, we have constructed a modest experience to demonstrate all the truths of my philosophy, in particular regarding the body, the soul and the union between them.

Your humble servant,

René Descartes

The girl's gaze remains fixed on the dancing pen of the philosopher.

A murmur seeps into his dream. One word, *Papa*, just as Rêver taught her. He wakes with a start to find himself ship-wrecked on the shore of his own consciousness. In an oversight, he has left the stove door open. The machine huddles inside, eyes pointing in his direction. Descartes tries to cling to the world with the sound of his voice.

'I know you are not my child, but an artifice without a soul.'

At any time, Anneke could walk in and see it. He must be more careful. He should get more sleep and return to the habit of thinking in bed in the mornings. For a while now, the first light of dawn has found him awfully awake amid a crowd of thoughts raging inside him. Most are not even his own thoughts but the voices of his enemies and so-called disciples, who trumpet distortions of his philosophy across the universities of Europe.

The sad truth is that no one has fully understood anything he has written.

The automaton takes to loitering in his room at night. Things are left out of place, which he attributes to Anneke's carelessness. Books and papers change position. The chair is placed a few steps away from the desk when he always pulls it close after work.

One day, upon waking up, he picks up the fresh scent of burning oil and spots an open book on the desk: the *Ars magnetica* of Athanasius Kircher, which Mersenne sent him. It is the only book in his possession other than the Bible and the *Summa theologiae* of Saint Thomas Aquinas. Descartes had considered giving the *Ars* to the servants to light the fire.

He sits on the edge of the bed and adjusts his nightgown. In its hiding place, the machine has changed position. Its head is tilted to one side, and its right hand is raised in the air in an unfinished gesture. This time he clearly remembers closing the door.

He approaches slowly. Illusions tend to fade as the mechanisms that produce them are observed more closely, but here is the opposite: the illusion becomes more perfect the more it is examined in detail.

The girl turns her head, and her eyes contemplate him. He closes the door and goes back to bed, but sleep is slow to return. The sound of the machine's breathing seems agitated and expectant. Autumn is coming and he must find another hiding place for it. The machine still wears the clothes Rêver gave it, and the dress is dirty and wrinkled.

Her soft, warm voice wakes him.

'Why don't you have books? What a curious thing, a philosopher without books.'

It is morning already. He must have fallen fast asleep. There were dreams that he does not remember, and it takes some time to decide that this is not one of them.

'Do you deign to speak now?'

'I was afraid that if I did, you would decide to hide me forever.'

'Have you been reading my letters too?'

'There isn't much else to read. Forgive me, father.'

'I'm not your father. Do not address me that way.'

Anneke's footsteps halt for a moment in front of the bedroom door. He stands still, waiting. Then the footsteps continue, and the residence is populated with the usual sounds: the washing of floors, the shaking of rugs, the clang of pots. Descartes examines the patina of dust on the edges of the desk, the window frames and the marble table beside the bed.

'If you want to go out at night, be careful that the servants don't see you.'

The machine watches him. He lingers for a moment, perhaps waiting for an answer, then he heads off for breakfast.

He scrutinises the blank page, his soul empty of words. His fingers squeeze and reshape the piece of wax. If he looks hard enough, the fibres that make up the paper suggest strokes, like a palimpsest of words rising to the surface. If only he could follow those lines.

The machine speaks, pulling him from a deep stupor.

'How long do you think you can hide me?'

She emerges slowly from the stove. She sticks her legs out, then her head. She looks at her hands and spreads out her fingers.

'I want to see the light of day, to feel it on my face. I want to play at being a real girl.'

'It is impossible. Everyone will suspect what you are.'

'Do you suspect it?'

'Of course. I have created you and therefore I know what you are.'

'Your argument is circular. Knowing that something is a plant, we can attribute plant-like qualities to it, even when the plant has decided to walk and talk. That doesn't prove anything. If you didn't previously know what I am, could you tell the difference? Come on, father, I have noticed the way you look at me. I remind you of your daughter.'

'Maybe, but just for a moment. That doesn't prove any-thing. You couldn't fool people for long. Let me explain. While reason is a universal instrument that can be used in all kinds of situations, artificial bodies need a different arrangement for each particular action. A machine faithfully designed to mimic our bodies and actions could never use words or manipulate signs, as we do, to declare our thoughts to others. A machine could not give an adequate response to what is said in its presence, as the clumsiest of men can. Second, even though these machines could do some things the way we do, or perhaps even better, they would inevitably fail at others, which would show that they were acting not through understanding, but only through the arrangement of their organs.'

'I propose, then, that we solve this question by means of an experientia. Isn't that what I am, an experiment? It would be a game that would allow me some freedom. My proposal is the following—are you listening? You can ask me all the questions you want, for as long as you deem necessary. If I can't answer you in an adequate way or if something in my behaviour makes you suspect that I don't have the use of reason, as do those real men you talk so much about, then you win the game and I'll go back to my hiding place.'

'Very soon, your dispositions will not be sufficiently complex, and our conversation will be over.'

'But what if eternity wasn't long enough to exhaust all possible combinations of the machine? What if the conversation lasted your whole life? I will be left alone and sad, and you will go to the grave without knowing whether your entire philosophy is true or false.'

'Of course, my philosophy is true! I don't need experimental demonstration of it. Only God could create a machine of such subtle and ingenious mechanisms. Even animals are machines of this type, more refined than human art could ever conceive.'

'So what difference does it make? You will have someone to play cards with! Please, papa, let's try it.'

'Your abilities are evidently amazing. Maybe you could convince simple people.'

'I just want to convince you. Now, what do you think of Rêver's proposal?'

'Have you been listening to our conversations all this time?'

'Well, of course. They are your corporeal ideas, René. Can I call you that, René? If we're going to pretend that I'm Baroness de Rêver, or whoever, I'm going to need new dresses.'

'I will entrust Pietr with the procurement of clothing, shoes and whatever else. He will need your dress and shoes to judge the appropriate sizes.'

'Is he trustworthy?'

'Yes. He won't ask questions or discuss this with anyone.'

'I also need a name. I've already decided that after reading your Bible.'

Descartes watches her without blinking.

'My name is Eva, of course! Like her, I'm an artifice, and what is human art but the imitation of divine mechanics?'

Descartes agrees to play the game, on the condition that they establish strict rules. She will speak in public only when necessary and must be courteous and distant with the servants. Also, Helena must not see her, at least for now. This last consideration worries him more than any other.

They settle with ease into their respective roles, and soon a routine begins to develop. She learns to write in the morning while he reads or writes. Then, during the philosopher's lunch and walk, she practices embroidery in the main room while Anneke cleans the other rooms.

With the change of season, the mid-afternoon offers the best light. Descartes undresses her, opens the cover on her back and studies the mechanisms inside. He asks her to perform different movements, studying the tubes as they swell and exhale, forming a rhythmic loom in time with her movements.

He asks Eva to repeat a series of randomly chosen words and watches the silk lungs tapping against the ribs of bronze. At night they talk, continuing the game, the experience.

'So, René, the fact that we have the experience of thinking—is that not a fact of experience?'

'I thought I was the one asking the questions.'

'You won't be able to convince me that I don't have a soul. It is an obvious fact to me, clearly perceptible to my senses. I think, therefore I am.'

'Do you know who you are, my girl? Do you know *what* you are? How could you without the use of reason?'

'If I cannot ascertain that I am a thinking being based on the evidence of my own experience, then neither can you.'

Descartes rehearses the arguments that he will later develop in his responses to Princess Elizabeth. In many ways, Eva has proven to be helpful to him. In less than a week of practice, she has learned to imitate the philosopher's handwriting to perfection. Descartes can now attend to the correspondence without getting out of bed, while the machine reads incoming letters aloud and takes dictation in a perfectly articulated, melodious tone.

'Here I sleep for ten hours every night, without a worry to keep me awake. In my dreams, my mind wanders endlessly among groves, gardens and enchanted palaces, where I taste all the pleasures that are told in fables. Then gradually I intermingle my daydreams with my night dreams, and when I realise that I am awake, it only makes my happiness more perfect, and I allow my senses to share it, for I am not so austere as to deny my senses anything that a philosopher could grant them without offending their conscience.'

The machine pauses.

'Let's see, papa. Where do your thoughts go when you don't think? If the essence of the soul is thought, then we must be thinking all the time, and clearly this is not true.'

'I believe that the soul is always thinking, for the same reason that I believe that light always shines, although there are not always eyes to see it. Every night we have a thousand thoughts, and even when we are awake, we have a thousand thoughts in the course of an hour, not a trace of which remains in our memory. Whatever constitutes the nature of a thing always belongs to it. So, it would be easier for me to believe that the soul ceases to exist when we supposedly stop thinking than to conceive that the soul exists without thought.'

And so on, until the oil and wax emit their last breath.

He must admit that the girl is behaving wonderfully and that he enjoys her company. He is no longer afraid to capitulate to appearance, to give in to simulation. He is like an actor who believes in the reality of his role and the illusory world of the play, and he has always been attracted to, even passionate about, that image. An actor lives hidden from everyone's eyes.

Baroness de Chanteleux begins to take on tasks and responsibilities around the house. She picks fresh flowers and sets them on the tables and shelves. She helps the servants with the preparation of meals. Anneke and Ludolf are amazed that a Baroness deigns to peel potatoes, but they accept her like a daughter. The Baroness accompanies Descartes on his visits around the neighbourhood where he praises the ox someone has bought, or toasts the health of a new-born, or offers medical advice. On weekends they go to mass and then stroll through the markets. Eva is happy walking with him, arm in arm in broad daylight. They examine the products of the fair and stop to see the works of the traveling theatre groups.

In this manner, they hide their deception in plain view. Once a week, Descartes organises a dinner at the house. After dessert, they sing psalms. Everyone praises the girl's crystal voice and perfect tone. They are amazed that she knows all the psalms by heart. Rêver has prescribed the automaton a diet of peaches, pears, apples and figs. Descartes explains to them that the Baroness suffers from a health complication that must be treated with a strict diet.

Descartes teaches her how to care for the garden, including the principles of pruning, and how to judge the maturity of different fruits. In the afternoons, he imparts anatomy and geometry lessons for no more than two hours, as the Jesuits recommend. The girl learns quickly. She can draw straight lines without a ruler and perfect circles without a compass. She can solve problems by applying the principles of analytical geometry that her father invented, expressing geometric figures and problems in algebraic terms. As the sun sets, while they wait for the servants to retire, they play cards in the main room, and Descartes teaches her the tricks he learned in Paris.

Despite all this, he is aware that this game cannot last forever. A veil of anxiety covers him, palpable and elusive at the same time, a muddy turmoil at the bottom of the rivers of his soul. Next summer, the so-called Baroness de Chanteleux must return to her imaginary castle, and it will be time to put her back in her hiding place for a while.

In late spring, the omen arrives that Descartes has been waiting for. The machine is discovered. As he feared, Helena is the only one who recognises the automaton for what it is. The worst part is that, in a moment of weakness, he breaks in front of her, admitting the truth in an imprecise and stammering way.

Although he relies on Helena's discretion, it is time to go. They will move further north, to Egmond-Binnen. He has already made enquiries.

'Will you let me go out in our new house? Can we live this happy out in the open?'

'We'll see. Now you must prepare for the journey. You will be comfortable in the trunk with your pillows and dresses.'

'It's dark in there.'

'Just rest. And sleep.'

'I had a dream, René! It is my first dream, or at least the first one I remember.'

'And what have you dreamed, my girl?'

'I dreamed I was playing with you. We clapped our hands and made a rhythm with our palms and knees. We had to copy each other's patterns. What is happening?'

'It's a game I used to play with Francine.'

'I can dream! And isn't dreaming a form of thought? Have I won the challenge then?'

'I don't think so! Your nature has been discovered, therefore it is you who has lost the challenge. Now, what am I going to do with you? And where is that vermin Rêver hiding?'

'Come on, papa. Helena did not suspect the truth because of my behaviour. She discovered our game because I reminded her of your daughter, God shelter her in His heart! Helena made a very accurate deduction. Helena knows you well. Anyway, no one else will find out the truth. I will win the challenge, you'll see! You will take me to Paris, won't you? We will make a lot of money playing cards in the salons.'

'Come on, my girl. Time to start collecting our things. We must go to sleep early. Tomorrow you will come with me in the carriage. I've even been saving, especially for you, the books that Mersenne sent me from Paris. Very soon we will announce that my niece will come to spend a season in my new residence. How about that?'

'I'd like that very much, Uncle René!'

16

Which recounts the sorrowful end of the great philosopher René Descartes.

In 1649, Descartes entrusts his close friends with a series of detailed instructions on what to do with his debts, his unpublished writings and his correspondence. He visits Amsterdam and organises a farewell banquet with his Dutch friends. They sing psalms and have a few too many drinks. Descartes hides the automaton in a trunk, and at night, when they are alone, the machine taps the lid gently, begging to be let out, but he can't risk discovery by his host.

In September of that year, he departs for Stockholm by ship, to the court of Queen Cristina. The journey is tortuous, endless, taking place in a grey, empty and silent landscape. Descartes decides to remove her from the trunk regularly to avoid the now unbearable company of his own thoughts.

Voices are heard coming from his cabin. Rumours circulate among the crew. It's said that one voice belongs to Descartes, the other to a woman or girl. One sailor says he can hear a third, deep and raspy, with a strange accent.

His thoughts grow heavy in the raw, deep cold that seems to seep out from within his bones. Even the light seems to freeze in mid-air. Static beams, perfectly rectilinear, pierce a uniform sky without properties, like the vacuum dreamed of by the ancient atomists. Locked in his cabin, a small room reserved for officers, Descartes remains as still as possible, although his rest is not absolute since the ship moves at a constant speed over the waters.

He has requested that his meals be served in his cabin. One night, the Captain himself brings dinner and peeks around the room. The philosopher speaks to him about the problem of calculating longitude and how positions can be located on a map using a coordinate system. The Captain nods, feigning interest.

Descartes notices the Captain sneaking glances at the trunk where the automaton hides. This makes him a bit nervous, but he is taking all possible precautions. He lets her out for two hours in the morning and two at night. He closes the curtains before taking her out of the trunk, and they spend most of their time playing cards and talking in whispers.

The next evening, she says, 'I'm ready to continue our game. What will you ask me this time?'

'I'm not in the mood today, but you can read me something if you want.'

'Then you will hear your own thoughts reflected as in a mirror.'

'I see myself reflected in you, my dear. You are my mirror, my shadow.'

'I would like to draw another portrait of you, but for that I must see you in the lamplight. Why do you always think in the dark? You should put on your wig.'

'I'm tired. I'm done playing for today. You will see me like this, as I am.'

'Really? Is this, what I see, what you are? You look younger in the light. It's like time hasn't passed, like we're in Deventer or Amersfoort, remember?'

'I don't know if I remember anymore, or if I merely imagine. Over time, the theatre of memory grows vast and inscrutable, and the stage fills with more and more shadows. Or maybe it's me who's becoming smaller.'

'Will you keep me out tonight?'

'No. You saw how the Captain pokes around the cabin.'

'Don't worry. Nobody will find out. I'll be quiet as a mouse.'

'We can't take that risk. We are surrounded by ruffians and superstitious sailors.'

'I don't like that box. It's dark and I can't breathe.'

'You'll be out soon when we arrive in Stockholm. Once at the Queen's court, you can walk freely and do whatever you like. We will be in the company of enlightened people, and everyone will marvel at you. They will bow and greet you like a princess. I don't say "queen" because the court already has a queen, one possessing more knowledge, intelligence and reason than all the learned scholars and men of the Church back in the land where we once resided. You know, the French are shocked that Queen Cristina only takes fifteen minutes to dress, like a man. The Queen has also ordered the construction of a theatre. I want to write a play for the stage and maybe you can act in it.'

'Why are we going to such a cold and dark place? What are you really looking for there? You, who have grown up in the gardens of Touraine, where you first tasted the freedom of reason. Look at you now. Who are you trying to fool? Or perhaps you're trying to fool yourself. We need to go back to Holland, to the peace we enjoyed in those lands. Do you think the chatter of theologians and critics will not reach you on the other side of this sea?'

A sound interrupts the conversation. He turns to the window and thinks he sees a shadow behind the curtain. They remain silent until the shadow retreats. Now all they hear is the grinding of pulleys, the complaint of sails, the rattling of ropes against masts.

'It's time for you to go back to your hiding place,' says Descartes, avoiding the automaton's gaze. 'I'll leave the lid open. If you want, I can read you a story to help you sleep. I have some books by Ovid and Aeschylus.'

'Thanks, papa. I would like that. Read me the story of Ovid in which the woman is transformed into a tree. You'll release me tomorrow as soon as you wake up, alright?'

The days drag without logical succession or any sense of passing time. On the few occasions when Descartes goes to the deck, he is plagued by the feeling of being watched. Sensing that the sailors are looking at him suspiciously, he makes sure to come out with his cape and sword, his gloved hand ready on the hilt. It is difficult to sustain the notion of day and night in this twilight where sky and sea merge. He takes mental note of the hours on the clock face and the arrival of meals. On that artificial night when most of the crew is sleeping, the dialogues with the girl provide his only contact, his only source of consolation.

'You are exhausted from all your fights with those theologians and academics,' she reproaches him. 'Your gaze has become cloudy and distant. That fight with Voetius—why did you play along, father? Given enough time, these charlatans would have torn each other apart like hungry dogs.'

'For a long time, I found the peace I was looking for in Holland. There I took refuge in the solitude necessary for thinking and writing, away from all theological conflicts, but no peace lasts a thousand years. The professors who try to destroy me will gain more power to the point where the situation becomes intolerable.'

'I don't understand, and sometimes I think you don't either. Are you running away because of money problems? You went to Paris to look for that pension and came back empty handed.'

'Paris! The honour that I deserve in my own country has been denied me. They made fun of me, Francine. In Sweden I will have the public recognition that I deserve.'

'However, you hesitated a long while before deciding to come. The Queen dispatched a general to find you, and you sent him back home. And look at us now, on this cargo ship! In Sweden, your thoughts will ice up in mid-air and shatter on the ground.'

'I'm convinced that there is an attitude of the mind towards the physical that allows us to overcome all the unhappiness of life. Just as the sad stories that we see performed on stage often entertain us as much as the happy ones, in the same way the noblest souls derive an inner satisfaction from everything that happens to them, even the most painful and unbearable events. When they feel pain in their bodies, noble souls try hard to bear it, and this display of their own strength brings them satisfaction.'

'You have a convenient explanation for everything! But I'm not convinced. I can see in your face that you now regret granting women the same reasoning capacity as men!'

A weak, sharp laugh bursts from his lungs. 'You're not giving up, Francine. Remember that you are not a woman.'

'I like it when you call me Francine. Eva was a very unimaginative reference, I admit.'

Descartes stares at his letters, avoiding her. The girl insists.

'But I *think* and I'm sure of it. Knowing that I think is, in fact, itself a thought. Isn't that right? Father, why are you stubborn? Can't you see that what I'm saying is true? You created me for this. I'm your great experience. Now you can confirm, without room for doubt, that the mind is an effect of the corporeal machine and that therefore we cannot know anything except material appearances.'

'That's the thesis of Regius. Don't remind me. No, I love you for what you are. You are the creation of men, perhaps the most amazing thing that human art has ever devised. My soul is tired, and it can no longer hold on against the passions. It's as though by giving you life, you've taken some of my own.'

Again, a flurry of shadows. They remain motionless, silent. A third figure appears in the cabin, or perhaps it has always been there. The flickering light reveals the features of a man of indeterminate age. He could be a young libertine, a jeune vieux, or an elderly man jealously preserving his appearance. At first Descartes is reluctant to admit the fact of his presence.

The man speaks. 'I have come to say goodbye, my friend. It is the last time we will see each other in this life. Perhaps you will convince me to play one last game of Swiss tarot, or do you prefer lansquenet?'

'You deign to visit me after all this time.'

'I'm not the one who decides these things, Renatus. I don't even know what to call you anymore! Reyner Jochems, Cartelius, Carolas Zolindius, Duperron, René le Poitevan, Polybius, Renatus Cartesius. You have been all of them and none. On the contrary, I have not had any proper name. I'm merely a brief mention in one of your most famous writings. Brief but haunting. We could argue that your entire philosophical project revolves around me—I, who am only known for one thing: deceptor, mechanicus, demiurge.'

'You are Urganda the Stranger, the witch of the *Amadis Gaula*, who never appears twice with the same face.'

'How ironic, then, that the path to Truth must first pass through me.'

'Don't give yourself big airs. You are a provisional hypothesis, nothing more.'

'Like the hypothesis of the immateriality of the mind?'

'Leave him alone!' says the girl.

Descartes turns his attention to the cards on the table. He stares at them for a long time, his eyes closing.

The automaton takes the cards and skilfully shuffles them. 'Papa is falling asleep. Do you want to join the game?'

The man handles a piece of wax between his fingers.

'Oh Francine, he's just pretending to sleep, but he's listening to us with attention. Descartes, we could go on like this forever, you and I. We're made for each other! However, life is short. The crouching shadows gather at the doorway, and there is little time left. You will die an unheroic death, but the Work must go on. Are you still awake?'

'Nowadays I am awake even when I sleep.'

Francine raises her hand in a warning gesture. 'Let him sleep.'

'Fine. That's all, in any case. Good evening. It has been a pleasure'.

The interloper places the finished wax figurine on the table. It is in the shape of a man.

One night, a junior sailor, his curiosity fuelled by the rumours of other voices, peeks through the window of Descartes's cabin. Trembling, he appears before the Captain, announcing that he has seen a diabolical apparition in the room. He describes it as some kind of machine in the form of a girl. He says that he saw the philosopher bending over it, examining its exposed mechanisms, before the machine turned its head. Its gaze, cold and menacing like an eagle's, was fixed directly on the intruder.

The next day, the crew meets on deck, demanding that the Captain investigate the strange events taking place in the philosopher's cabin. The Captain invites Descartes to lunch in his quarters; however, before he can express the cause of his concern, a group of sailors, cabin boys and officers break in and discover the diabolical toy in the trunk. Apparently, it is sleeping.

The girl opens her eyes, staring at her executioners without expression. The illusion is so perfect it instils terror. A creature summoned from the depths of Hell itself, surely the product of black magic, the dark arts. Who knows how many demons and evil spirits have been invoked to inhabit that piece of soulless matter! At first no one dares to approach it, but eventually the men overcome their fear and pounce on the machine. They carry her to the deck as the girl struggles weakly.

Alerted by the commotion, Descartes and the Captain emerge. Taking stock of the situation, Descartes draws his sword and demands that the sailors hand over the creature to him at once, but they manage to contain him and the automaton is promptly thrown overboard. Instantly and without trace, it disappears below the surface of the icy water.

Descartes raises a cry of pain to the sky, as though he has been stabbed. Amid the din, no one notices the figure of a well-dressed man, of imprecise age and large, misshapen hands, observing the situation from the foot of the mainmast.

Shortly after arriving at the court of Queen Cristina of Sweden, the Queen summons Descartes to impart philosophy classes in the library at five in the morning. He regrets the decision to come, as he is not in his element there. He misses his loneliness, without which it is difficult to progress on the path to Truth.

He catches the flu in the residence where he is staying, the abode of the French ambassador Pierre Chanut. After more than a week of high fever, and already very weak, Descartes finally agrees to be bled. His mind fills with dreams, memories, chimeras, and there is no longer any point in trying to tell them apart.

Before going to Heaven, men spend time in bed, preparing to leave. They become smaller and paler, and their gazes already seem to contemplate that other place. People gather around to pray for their souls.

The doctor arrives, then the priest and members of the court.

The main architect of the rationalist worldview of modern science and technology is buried in an unnamed grave in the cemetery of an orphan's hospital. He rests alongside the bodies of unbaptised children, plague victims and kindred homeless souls.

History will portray his death as Christian and devout, but, really, Death is the same for all beings: the horizon of naked reality, preceding all individuality.

EPILOGUE

The blanket of snow stretches to the horizon, rimmed by a forest of skeletal, leafless trees. The sky is grey and still. Across the plain walks a small figure, his footsteps perfectly imprinted on the snow. The distance between the steps becomes shorter until he falls headfirst, exhausted, and the landscape is still again.

A few moments pass, then two figures enter the scene—a broad-shouldered man and a young girl. They walk leisurely toward the dark bundle in the snow, breaking the eternal calm and transmuting it into time.

The waves slow down as the mechanisms exhaust their momentum. She thinks she is dead. The sound of footsteps is heard in the gloom.

ACKNOWLEDGEMENTS

Firstly, my deep gratitude to John Sutton, my PhD supervisor, who ignited my passion for Descartes. Also, my eternal thanks to Sofía Suez for her love, encouragement and tireless impetus.

It would be pointless to thank all the literary sources that were plundered in the making of this book, but some were particularly important: *Descartes: A Biography*, by Desmond Clark (2005), and *Cogito, ergo sum: The life of René Descartes*, by Richard Watson (2002).

Finally, thank you to my editor, dear friend and unconditional fan, Simon Sellars, for his meticulous work on the manuscript.

ABOUT THE AUTHOR

Andrés Vaccari is the author of *Robotomy* (Saturn Press, 1997), *Smoky: Relato de Muerte, Exilio y terror* (Borde Perdido, 2022), *El Enjambre y las Sombras* (EMB, 2018, Regional Narrative Award), *Hypercapitalism and Other Tales of Planetary Madness* (Wanton Sun, 2023), *Suicidados* (Diotima, 2024) and *Even Animals Are Machines* (Wanton Sun, 2024; originally published as *La Pasión de Descartes*, Barenhaus, 2019). He is also the author of two stage plays and a multimedia performance piece, *Nothing Here But Shadows*, 2019-2024.

He obtained his Doctorate in Philosophy from Macquarie University with a thesis on Descartes and the links between posthumanism and mechanistic biology. He has worked for universities in Australia and Argentina, as researcher, lecturer and tutor. His academic papers and short stories have appeared in various international journals and magazines.

Find out more about his work at www.andresvaccari.com.

ALSO BY ANDRÉS VACCARI

Ghost hunters in the Middle East. Lonely suburbanites who worship machines. Sentient, bloodthirsty insects invading the planet by stealth. Cyborg media barons and a new type of asymmetric warfare. All populate the astonishing short stories of Andrés Vaccari.

Collected in *Hypercapitalism and Other Tales of Planetary Madness*, Vaccari's worlds are disturbing and unpredictable.

Part science fiction, part horror, part speculation, these delicate pieces of narrative engineering will make you think twice about looking in the mirror.

Hypercapitalism and Other Tales of Planetary Madness by Andrés Vaccari.

ISBN 978-0-6456543-3-2

www.wantonsun.com

ALSO FROM WANTON SUN

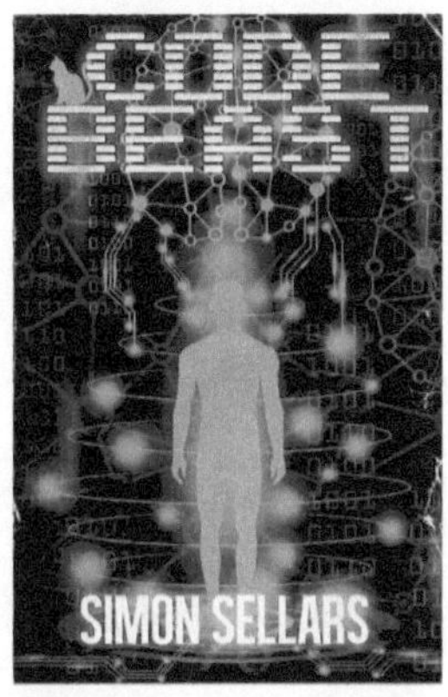

In the near future, Kalsari Jones is hooked on the Vexworld, a global mixed-reality network accessed through neural implants. As his addiction grows, he is plagued by sentient hallucinations and an urge to strip the flesh from his bones. At his lowest ebb, he must also face his latent digisexuality, an erotic attraction to artificial intelligence.

Seeking answers, he meets Ingram Ravenscroft, a cult leader claiming a treatment for digisexuality. Smitten, Kalsari allows his brain to be rewired, only for the operation to leave him with unwanted telepathic powers.

Lost in inner space, Kalsari angers a band of rogue AI who've escaped the Vexworld to seek refuge in the time-sinks of the fourth dimension. Battling the shapeshifting bots, he discovers the shocking truth about his virtual obsessions—and Ravenscroft's hidden role in the story of his life.

Code Beast by Simon Sellars

ISBN 978-0-6456543-1-8

www.wantonsun.com